Zax & Dax

Dennis Eaves

Lea
Street Press
Read. Imagine. Live.

For Zax...thanks for slaying the beasts.

Zax & Dax

Prologue

Deep on the edge of the milky way is a white hole, a singularity in a region of space-time. Nothing from the outside can enter this particular singularity, but energy-matter and light can escape. Within this specific white hole exists a vast source of pure energy that is emitting a continuous, extremely small amount—practically hair-thin—into space. But this energy is the farthest thing from light or purity; it is dark and can only be described as evil itself.

No one knows its source or its intentions. However, The Office has uncovered its destination, and that destination threatens the existence of all mankind.

Its target is Earth.

It has been almost a year since the bright, powerful energy lying in the core of the Earth bestowed its extraordinary powers on a teenage boy from Tacoma. His name is Zax, and he is the beast slayer. To date, he has destroyed three beasts: the Chupacabra, the Brute, and the Dark Matter, aka D.M., and, in a battle to save those he loves, he killed Professor Brian, the mad scientist who created them.

With the discovery of the dark energy, Zax must now confront this unknown evil and save the world from total annihilation.

Chapter 1
The Satellite

Part 1

"Zax, are you awake? We need you to come down."

Standing at the foot of the stairs, Jenny looked up the staircase and yelled. Her purple terry-cloth bathrobe was loosely tied at the waist, and her hands were tucked into the pockets.

Zax awoke from his sleep at the sound of Jenny's voice, and with his eyes still closed, he slid his hand from underneath his pillow and felt around on his nightstand for his phone to check the time. His alarm had not gone off yet, so he knew he had not overslept. Seeing that it was only 6:30, he pulled the sheet over his head. *Not now, Jenny.*

"Zax?"

Seriously? I still have fifteen minutes before I usually get up! "I am now," he mumbled to himself and sat up on the side of the bed. "Be there in a sec," he yelled back.

Zax stood up and pilfered through his laundry basket until he found a pair of workout shorts and a white t-shirt. It was too early to care if they were clean or not.

Whatever she wants to talk about can't be that important. I've got to leave for school by 7:30.

He grabbed his phone and headed downstairs.

As he stepped off the carpeted stairs onto the hardwood floor, he saw Ethan and Jenny sitting quietly in their brown, faux leather recliners. They were clutching their coffee mugs and facing the TV on the wall opposite the stairs. The arrangement of the living room formed a semi-circle in front of it. A white fabric sofa loaded with red and blue decorative pillows sat between the recliners and belonged solely to Zax most of the time. He only had to give it up when they had company. When other people popped in, he grabbed a stool from the kitchen for himself or just sat on the floor. Jenny always sat on the recliner to the right of the sofa; Ethan was always to the left.

"Sit down," Ethan said, motioning for Zax to take a seat. "We need to talk about something."

Still trying to wake up, Zax glanced over at Jenny. But even through his sleepy eyes, the look on her face told him that this was more than a "we love you and hope you have a great day" moment. He walked around Jenny and sat down in the center of the sofa.

"Um, ok?" Zax said, confused. Jokingly, he added, "This isn't another talk about the birds and the bees, is it?"

"What? No, of course not," Jenny said and took a sip of her perfectly blended coffee. With three teaspoons of sugar and one teaspoon of cream, neither he nor Ethan knew how she drank something so sweet first thing in the morning. "This is about your plans after high school."

Zax looked at her, puzzled. He had no idea where this was going or why.

Ethan lowered the footrest on his recliner and sat upright. "You need to decide if you're going to college or not and what you'll major in if you do. It's time to start thinking about what you want as a career. You need to start planning for your future," he said, getting straight to the point as usual.

Really? Are we having this conversation at 6:30 a.m.? Right now? Before a school day, he thought. Zax could not help but chuckle to himself at their timing. He sunk into the sofa pillows and stared at the ceiling.

"I know. I just don't know what I want to do. So I haven't given it much thought." *Can't we do this later? Like maybe after I fully wake up?*

"Well, you need to think about it," Jenny said curtly, taking another sip of her coffee. "I checked my email this morning and saw that I had one from your school. When I read it, it said they're having a career fair after school today. Since you didn't mention it—"

"We know it's not mandatory," Ethan butted in, "but you should at least check it out. Even though you have these extraordinary powers, you can still live a normal life. We're serious about this, Zax, and you should be too."

But what if I don't want a normal life? Zax thought. "Okay. I'll check it out if I can."

Despite what he'd just told Ethan and Jenny, he had actually spent a lot of time thinking about what he wanted to do. The problem was that he could never figure out exactly where his long-term interests lay. After he got his powers, he assumed he would start working at The Office and have a career there. But after their talk this morning, it seemed that might not be the case.

They sat silently for several minutes, each lost in their own thoughts. Zax had no idea what they were thinking, but for him, this was way too serious, way too early in the morning to be thinking or talking about.

Jenny glanced at the digital clock—which doubled as a weather station—on the entertainment center and realized it was almost seven. She turned back to Zax and nodded towards the stairs. "You've got to go get ready."

Zax looked at her smiling face, then got up and headed back to his room. As he stepped on the second tread, she said, "Hey, Zax." He stopped and looked back at her. "No matter what career path you choose, just know that we will always be proud of you."

He nodded. He knew she meant it. And there was no question in his mind that she and Ethan really and truly only wanted the best for him.

"I know," he said, then continued up the stairs to shower and get ready for his day.

As the hot water rained upon him, he thought about their conversation. Ethan and Jenny were right. It was time for him to begin making some decisions. He knew he had been given a special gift, and whatever he did, he hoped to use it to make a difference. But what that would be like, he didn't know.

I don't have any idea where I can work that my power will be of any use other than The Office, he thought as he rinsed the shampoo from his hair.

A few minutes later, he turned the water off and reached for his towel. Stepping out of the shower, he said aloud, "But I'll figure it out."

2

Zax waved to Jenny and Ethan as he backed his dark blue 2008 Chevy Malibu down the slightly inclined, slightly curved driveway and headed for school. Other than his backpack and a bottle of water, the inside of his car was immaculate. The light gray interior looked as though it had never been touched or sat on. The exterior was just as pristine. Though he did not want to admit it, he was a bit of a neat freak when it came to his car.

He had never expected to get a car so quickly and certainly never thought he'd have one as nice as the Malibu. He had calculated that he would have to save every dime he made for the next sixteen months just to afford a jalopy. But within three months of learning to drive and getting his license, he was driving a good-looking car that had been custom engineered for the powers he held, and it did not cost him a thing. Since it had been modified specifically for him, he knew he could drive to school, or anywhere, without blowing up a freeway. All this was thanks to Walter, the son of The Office's director.

Walter had purchased the Malibu several years earlier with the intent of refinishing it in his spare time. But for one reason or another, he never got around to it and eventually lost interest; that was, until Zax got his license and suddenly he knew where the Malibu belonged. It belonged with Zax. It was the least he could do after all the dangerous situations The Office had put him in.

"You deserve this, Zax," he said when he handed over the keys. "Not only did you destroy the beasts and Professor Brian, but you also saved lives. You're a real hero, you know."

Once Walter had made the decision to give the car to Zax, he tasked The Office's team of engineers to adapt and develop new technologies that would work with Zax's power, assuring he could not overload the vehicle. Ultimately, their redesign and reconfiguration of the car's entire electrical system surpassed their expectation. After replicating Zax's power for test purposes, their creation was a success. Zax now had a well-deserved car, made especially to meet his needs, and as a bonus, he no longer had to rely on Ethan or Jenny for a ride.

Zax pulled into the school parking lot five minutes later than usual and instantly wished that Jenny had read her email the day before.

If she'd just checked it yesterday, maybe we could've had our talk over dinner instead of this morning, and I could find a parking space! Frustrated, he circled the parking lot until he found an open space between a black Jeep Wrangler and a lime green Volkswagen Bug. He pulled into the space—the farthest out he'd ever had to park—and got out. "Oh well...I'm sure the walk will do me good."

He had never seen the parking lot so full, but then again, he was always there much earlier. He opened the back door on the driver's side and grabbed his backpack, locking the Malibu behind him.

Walking through the parking lot, he could see Mark and Jack in the distance. They were already at their usual hangout—the side entrance of the school, closest to the cafeteria. How and why the three of them had chosen that spot was anybody's guess. But without fail, they met in the same place every morning and chatted while waiting for the first bell to ring. When it did, they all went in different directions—Mark to chemistry, Jack to English, and Zax to pre-calculus.

When Zax got close enough to see what Mark was wearing, a huge grin came to his face. Plastered on Mark's dark purple t-shirt was a bright red ketchup bottle, running, with the words 'Ketch-Up' written underneath. "Hey Mark, I like your shirt."

"Thanks. Jack told me the same thing." He smiled jokingly and looked down at his shirt. "I've got to get more of these."

Zax shook his head, laughing. He glanced over to Jack. "I like yours too, Jack."

"Thanks, man. Seattle Seahawks rule. Well, maybe not this year."

They all burst out laughing.

Their laughter and joking continued for a few more minutes before Zax changed the subject. "Trying to find a parking space this morning was crazy."

Mark and Jack looked towards the crowded parking lot.

"I still can't believe you got your own car before me," Jack said, staring out across the sea of cars. "And it still feels like yesterday when I would call you Caveman."

"Yeah, and how Jaiden called you out for having a quarter of a brain," he said without missing a beat. "Speaking of cars, why are there so many today?"

"Hey, I'm not even on the football team anymore," Jack half-heartedly joked.

Quitting the team was not something Jack ever wanted to do. But when he could not stop his teammates from making fun of or teasing other kids, he felt he had no choice; he had to break away. By doing so, he created his own kind of rebellion and stood up for what he believed. Bullying was wrong. Period. And he refused to be a part of it. He hoped that, over time, some of the other players would do the same. None of them were good enough to get a college scholarship, anyway, including himself. Their coach had made that clear.

"I think it's because of career day," Mark said.

Behind them, a roaring laughter erupted. Zax nodded in the direction of the ruckus. "Sounds like your old pals are having fun."

Jack glanced over his shoulder and saw his former football buddies huddled around each other as if preparing for a play. *Idiots,* he thought. "I cannot believe I ever associated with those guys."

Mark could see how upset Jack was at the sight of the team and decided to redirect the conversation. He turned to Zax. "Speaking of Jaiden, hasn't it been about a year since you started dating?"

"Yeah, it's almost been a year since we had our first picnic at the pond," Zax said, smiling. "We still go over there every now and then for a date, but it's been a while."

And with that, the first bell rang. "Well, there it is," Mark said. "Just what we've been waiting for. Guess we should get moving before we're late."

"Yeah," Jack said, annoyed, still staring at the want-to-be jocks. "We should."

"See you two at lunch," Zax said as they parted ways. *And only an hour until I can see Jaiden!*

For the first two days of the school year, Jaiden had met Zax, Mark, and Jack before first period. But with her class being on the other side of campus, it was impossible for her to get to computer science on time. Two tries, two tardies. Since three tardies led to detention, she and Zax decided to wait and see each other after their first classes.

Their meeting place was outside the room where Professor Brian had attacked them—the room where Zax had first, unintentionally, used his power. But before he could see her, he had to survive an hour of pre-calc.

Zax navigated the busy hallway to Room 114. Pre-calculus was not his favorite class, but since his teacher, Mr. Jackson, basically gave all the answers to the problems, it wasn't that bad. He hoped college would be the same but seriously doubted it. The only challenge he found in class was waiting the fifty-six minutes until he could see Jaiden.

3

When class ended, Zax bolted out of his chair. He darted down the hallway and up the stairs. On the first day of school, he had staked his claim to the desk nearest the door. By doing so, he was able to get ahead of the students that cluttered the hallway and seemed to be in no hurry to get anywhere, especially their next class.

As he reached the top of the stairs, Zax saw Jaiden leaning against the wall smiling at him. Although he was always excited to see her, something about her today made him feel even more drawn to her. Whether it was because it was close to their one-year anniversary or if it was just a good day, he didn't know. And it didn't matter. He was just excited to see her.

"Hey," he said, leaning against the wall beside her. She had on jeans, a partially tucked black t-shirt, and a denim jacket. Her long hair was pulled back in a ponytail, making her eyes sparkle more than usual. To him, there was nothing more beautiful. *I still can't figure out how I got so lucky!*

"How was pre-calc?"

"Too slow if you ask me," he said, grinning.

"Yeah, I know what you mean. Same for computer science." She looked away for a moment, then turned back to him, blushing. "I couldn't stop thinking about you."

She's so cute when she blushes, he thought. "I couldn't stop thinking about you, either." Looking into her eyes, he was overcome by that nervous, indescribable feeling you get in your stomach when you see someone you love. All the memories they'd made over the past year flooded his mind.

"It's hard to believe it's been a year since we got together," Zax said.

"I know." Still smiling, she looked down at the floor as her own random memories of their time together filtered in.

A few seconds later, Zax decided to bring them back to the present. "Hey, did you hear about the career fair or career day or whatever it's called?"

"Oh yeah," she said, lifting her head. "Are you going? It's after school today, right?"

"Yeah, it's supposed to start at 5:00, but I don't know if I'm going. Jenny and Ethan said I should, but I don't really know what I want to do after we graduate. Or what I can do, for that matter. With my power..." His words trailed off, and he suddenly sounded discouraged.

"What if you went to work for The Office? I mean, you basically work there already. They'd be crazy not to hire you after all you've done for them. And they know what you're capable of. They know everything about you. Maybe you could talk to Walter and see what he thinks? They might even help pay for college if you wanted to go."

Zax looked at her and wished he had the confidence in himself that she had. "That might work. I assumed I couldn't since Ethan and Jenny didn't mention it. They only talked about the career fair," he said, feeling a bit more encouraged. "But you're right. They do know what I'm capable of. If they hired me, I would have unlimited access to The Office training rooms, which has to be a win for them. The training rooms at home are good, but they don't compare to the ones at The Office."

He paused for a moment, thinking as he listened to the chaos in the hallway. "I'm not sure what additional education I'd need to become an agent. Maybe something in defense or covert intelligence?" he asked rhetorically and shrugged his shoulders.

"See, that could work. I think it's a great plan!" Jaiden glanced at the clock hanging on the opposite wall. "Come on. We've only got a minute to get to study hall."

4

Study hall was three doors down in the two-story library. Checkered beige and green Berber carpet covered the entire room. The exterior wall faced east, and the floor-to-ceiling, wall-to-wall windows flooded the space with natural light and made the pale green walls seem reflective. It was rumored that Ms. Panilli, the librarian, had personally selected the décor in an attempt to bring the outdoors in.

Lining the windowed wall were twelve two-person round tables. Rectangular tables were situated between the book stacks in the middle of the room. Along the wall opposite the windows were computer workstations. If you showed up and kept your voice down, Ms. Panilli did not care where you sat, what you studied, or how much you talked. Everyone in school knew this was the easiest "A" to get.

Zax and Jaiden followed the other students into the library and went to their usual table, the small round top farthest from Ms. Panilli. Though there were no designated seat assignments, everyone migrated to the same spot every time they took a seat. Eight of the small tables were claimed with two students at each. The remaining students were scattered about, with the exception of Freddy Smith. Freddy preferred computers over people and stayed at the computer station furthest from the closest person to him.

Just as the tardy bell rang, Jaiden pulled her chair out and plopped her backpack on the floor. "I always wanted to be an author. Writing is one of the only ways I can truly express myself."

"Here," she answered as Ms. Panilli called her name and glanced over her shoulder, making sure she was heard. She turned back to Zax. "Sometimes I find myself trembling, even terrified, when I get too stressed. But when I start writing, it makes me feel better; it calms me down."

"Here," Zax responded. Rather than calling roll alphabetized by last name, Ms. Panilli called it by first. He was last.

"Kind of weird that we've never talked about this," Jaiden quietly and nervously laughed.

"Kind of, yeah." Zax leaned over the table, starting to feel concerned. "You know you can tell me if something is wrong. If you're worried about my powers getting out of control like they did back at the pond or anywhere else I seemed to have lost it, you don't need to. I have really been working on that for the past year, and I truly think I can manage it without creating havoc. But if there is any problem, in general, you can just talk to me."

She looked down at her clasped hands resting on the table. "I know. It's not that. It's just...I don't want to bother you. I mean, what Professor Brian said back at the castle, was right. If it weren't for me, you would still have a normal life."

"And what was it you said while we were there? 'If I didn't want to be with you, then I would have stayed away from the beginning,' or something like that."

He reached out and put his hands on top of hers. Jaiden lifted her head and met his eyes.

"Think of it this way. If you'd never given me your phone, Professor Brian would have killed me while I was in detention. So technically, you saved my life."

Jaiden stared at him until her eyes began to water. She pulled her hands from underneath his and wiped the tears away before they ran down her cheek.

"Are you ok?"

"I'm fine," she sniffled, trying to pull herself together. She knew she needed to change the subject before she descended into an emotional wreck. "Enough about that. Did you hear about the satellite drifting near Earth? The news said it launched years ago to take pictures of possible planets or galaxies near the edge of the milky way. They also said that it's been years since the scientists have heard anything from it, and now if it gets any closer, it could crash into the Pacific Ocean based on its current trajectory."

"Really?" he asked. Despite hearing about it a few days earlier, he decided not to let on. At this moment, it seemed the right thing to do. "I wonder if it still has some pictures and what was captured."

5

Forty-five minutes later, the bell rang for third period. They hugged and once again headed in opposite directions. Morning classes came and went, as did lunch and afternoon classes. When the final bell rang at three o'clock, they caught up again with Mark and Jack near the cafeteria, in the exact spot where they met before school.

"Hey Zax, what's up with this satellite I'm hearing about?" Jack asked as he and Jaiden approached. "I heard some of the kids talking about it. They said it may be heading into the Pacific Ocean."

"I don't know anything, really. I only know what everyone else knows, which is what the news has been saying," Zax said. "After I take Jaiden home, I'm going in and see what I can find out at The Office. They probably know more about it. I doubt it is that big of a deal, though. I think they would have gotten in touch with me if it were."

"Let us know when you know something," Mark said.

"I will."

Zax turned to Jaiden. "Ready?"

"Yeah. I think we're all anxious to hear what's happening, so the sooner you get to The Office, the better," she said. "Mark. Jack. See you tomorrow."

"See you," they said.

By the time Zax and Jaiden got to his car, the Jeep was gone. The VW was still there. Right then, he vowed that he would protest the next time Ethan and Jenny wanted to have a morning talk. Arriving later than usual and having to park so far away was not something he wanted to become a habit.

Though he had a standing offer to take Jack and Mark home after school, they opted to walk—rain or shine—since they lived only a few blocks away. They had tried it both ways and consistently found that it was faster for them to walk than hitch a ride. By the time they walked to the car, even when Zax had a good parking space, and waited for the other cars to get out, walking was faster. Ten minutes faster, to be exact.

6

After he dropped Jaiden off, Zax went straight to The Office. Most of his coworkers had stopped trying to kill him for the reward that the director had put on his head, but the few who refused to stop swore it was to help him train and to hone his skills and reflexes.

As he stepped into the reception area of the building, no one seemed to notice his entrance. Usually, at least one person, maybe two, saw him and went on the attack. But no bullets flew, and there were no obstacles to dodge. He walked to the elevator and took it up to the main meeting room. No one turned around as the elevator door opened. It was apparent something was going on; something was different.

The room was eerily silent. Everyone present was gathered on the north side of the room with their eyes fixed on the primary monitor. The monitor was mounted on the wall opposite the elevator and to the left of where he had entered.

Zax stood in the entryway for a few seconds before he saw Walter off to the side of the crowd; he looked terrified. Tiptoeing across the room, he stopped when he got to Walter.

"Hey Walter, what's wrong?" he whispered.

Startled, Walter jumped at the sound of his voice and looked over his shoulder. "Oh hey," he said, quickly turning his attention back to the monitor. "I'm sure you've heard about the satellite drifting towards Earth."

"I heard it on the news. Jaiden mentioned it, and I heard other people talking about it at school, but that's it. Why? What's going on?"

A heavy, ominous aura filled the room. Whatever was happening had to be bad news; you could cut the tension with a knife.

"We traced the satellite's trajectory, and it's going to land in the Pacific Ocean, just not in the water. It's going to land on Professor Brian's castle," Walter said, nodding at the continuous blip on the screen. "We took a closer look at the castle. Apparently, there has been a weak signal coming from it ever since you defeated Professor Brian. He must have turned it on secretly as soon as you entered his lab. I don't know how we've missed it until now. I mean, he did seem pretty sure that Dax was going to come and kill you. The castle has been acting as a tether for the satellite, pulling it closer and closer to Earth. It has been active ever since you defeated Professor Brian a year ago."

"Why would Professor Brian want to bring the satellite to Earth?" Zax asked.

"My guess is because of the deal he made with…whatever that thing is, that's in the white hole. We have a scan running on the satellite to see if it has the same properties as the ooze we collected from Professor Brian's experiments at the castle. We should get the results any second now."

Zax didn't know what to make of all this. He closed his eyes, and in a weakened voice, he said, "So, if the scan comes back positive, that would mean Dax—the thing that Professor Brian was talking about, the thing that is supposed to kill me—could be here?"

Suddenly the monitor turned red, and a blaring, high-pitched noise filled the room. In a matter of seconds, the results were in, and "98 percent match" flashed across the screen.

Zax's eyes popped open at the sound of the piercing noise, and his pupils became dilated. Unable to take his eyes off the screen, he was instantly overcome with fear. His heart began racing. The energy started to seep from his body due to all the emotions swirling inside him—fear, concern, stress, worry.

Trembling, he mumbled, "Dax, h-he is here, isn't he?"

Walter took a deep breath and put his hand on Zax's shoulder. "We don't know yet. We have a team of agents going to the castle to check it out. But if it turns out to be him, then we're all going to be in trouble."

"It's him. I don't know how, but I can feel an intense darkness coming from the satellite. I know it's miles away in the sky, but somehow, I can feel the intensity coming from it."

Zax stood, rigid and frightened. More and more energy began escaping his body.

"We should know something soon," Walter said calmly, hoping to ease Zax's anxiety. "The agents are prepping to leave for the castle as we speak. The best thing we can do right now is to stay positive."

Zax began to feel weak. Even though he had not used much energy recently and had plenty, he suddenly felt like every ounce had been sucked from his body, completely depleted. He collapsed and fell to the floor. The room around Zax and Walter became strangely still, as if time had come to a complete halt.

"Zax!" Walter shouted.

Zax began to move. Slowly rising to a standing position, he opened his eyes. When he did, the blue eyes he once had, were gone. There was no longer a pupil; there was no longer an iris. There was nothing but a solid yellow glow where his blue eyes had been.

Walter stumbled backward in shock.

"No! You cannot send any humans to check out the crash site. If you do, they will ultimately die." A strange, deep, unrecognizable voice came from Zax's mouth.

"I am the energy; I have taken control of Zax's body, and I can explain everything that is about to happen."

"W-what do you mean? What is happening?" Walter asked franticly. "What is about to happen?!"

"Quite possibly, the end of the world, more or less," the energy said.

Dennis Eaves

Chapter 2
The Truth

Part 7

"What do you mean, 'the end of the world'?!" Walter asked, still frantic. He looked down at the floor where Zax had fallen. "And what happened to Zax!"

"It's what it sounds like. The world could be on the brink of destruction. As for Zax, he is still conscious. We are one and the same, but I took control over him by linking to the energy he possesses in his body because I know the truth behind the relationship between Zax and Dax," the energy said. "I can't get into all the specific details about that right now, but I can tell you why no human should get near Dax. May I continue?"

Walter stood stunned at the entity in front of him. Apart from its eyes and voice, it looked exactly like Zax. Trying to process this scenario, he calmly, yet not so confidently, agreed. He knew that in order to get the most information possible, he had to collect himself, accept this surreal moment, and, most importantly, stay focused.

"Ok," he said. "But after you tell me why we can't get near Dax, you're going to tell us everything. And that includes telling Zax why he is the one that possesses your power."

"Of course, I wouldn't have it any other way. Dax's power is much stronger than mine, or well, Zax's. His power can manipulate lower-intelligent humans and make them do his bidding. You would have to be on an Einstein level to keep from falling under his control. He has been doing it for billions of years. Every wrongdoing or mishap from the beginning of time has been by the hand of Dax and his power. Everything bad that's ever happened—from robbing a bank to starting a war—is because of him."

"Ok, so basically, you're saying that Dax has the power of bad influence?"

"In a way, yes. It's not really mind control, but if anyone gets near him or his energy, they will be affected by his negative power and start to behave in a negative way. But his power cannot affect Zax in that fashion. The best way you can describe his power is that it's the ultimate evil."

"What? Like the devil?"

"Dax does tend to be mistaken as a devil or demon or some kind of dark entity by some, but believe me, you would prefer he was one if you had to battle him, that is. He is, at his core, a brutal, ruthless entity. Zax, on the other hand, or well, me and Zax, are the exact opposite of Dax and his power. We can't control anyone or their decisions in life, at least not in the state we are in now."

"What do you mean 'in the state you are in now'? Were you once stronger? Can you get stronger?"

"Yes, to both questions, but that is a story for another time."

"Ok," Walter sighed, frustrated. He ran his hand through his hair and looked around at the perfectly still room. *What now?* he thought.

A few seconds later, he turned his attention back to the energy possessing Zax. "So what do we do about Dax if we can't get near him? If I send my agents to the site and Dax is there, they'll be killed by his diabolical, evil power. Correct?"

"Not necessarily. But they will never be the same person again. For all practical purposes, they will be dead to you."

"What about Zax? Is it possible to send him to deal with Dax, or would he be in danger as well?"

"Zax would not be in danger because Dax is too weak right now to take any defined form. Dax doesn't have the capability to kill him or even attempt to attack him. But his power is still genuine, and any human getting close would be fiercely affected."

"If he's weak, shouldn't we send Zax to destroy him before he gets any stronger? Maybe even before he crashes?" Walter asked.

"I'm afraid that's not possible either. Dax knows he is weak right now, so as soon as he lands at the castle, he will make his way through the earth's crust into a safe place and hibernate until he becomes more powerful.

"With regards to destroying him before he lands…he will probably have a shield of his energy to protect him as he enters the atmosphere, as well as from Zax. The shield would prevent his destruction from the crash or any attack."

Walter remained silent.

"There is one other thing you should know about Dax that makes him terrifying beyond his vile powers," the energy continued. "He is a genius on how to get his way. Suppose you were to send an agent to investigate. In that case, it's entirely possible that Dax would take over that agent's body and pump energy into it until it became so powerful that he could—and would—return on a mission to kill everyone here, including Zax. And he'd do it before you knew what hit you."

"What do we do then? Just sit around and wait for him to kill us?"

"Of course not. Dax is survival smart, and I am, or well, Zax is battle smart. Zax will train with the energy he uses and make weapons, defenses, and other strategic objects. He will also learn the proper strategy for battle. I, the energy, have significant knowledge on Dax's weaknesses, and Zax has the skills necessary to use the energy. He hasn't even scratched the surface of what he can do yet. He needs to be trained to the bone.

"I will now let Zax have control of his body again. No need to tell him everything we just talked about. He heard it all."

The energy closed its eyes, and when they reopened, Zax and his blue eyes had returned. Motion returned to the room around them as if nothing had happened. Time had been suspended.

8

"Zax?" Walter asked. "Are you ok? You heard all that, right?"

"Yeah," he said, feeling unsteady. "It sounds like Dax is here, and I am the only one who even remotely has a chance of beating him."

Zax's mind began spinning as Professor Brian's final words blared inside his head. *"Dax is coming for you!"* He had heard these words every day since his victory over Professor Brian, but never this loud and never this threatening. Professor Brian's premonition seemed to be materializing; his prediction was finally coming true. The fear he had suppressed and now faced, flooded him all at once.

He closed his eyes and took a deep breath. He knew he had to fight through the fear of those haunting words. *"Dax is coming for you!"*

"Well, you heard the energy," Walter said, shifting to a ready-for-action tone. He could see the fear in Zax and decided the quickest way to get rid of it was to appear unconcerned. He wasn't sure it would work but thought it was worth a try. "It's time to start your advanced training. We don't have any choice but to equip you better."

Are you kidding? Zax thought as he stared at Walter. *I'm a high school student. What do they expect of me?* Then, he slowly began to grasp the magnitude of the situation. *Relax Zax, you need to work through it,* he told himself. *Think of Jaden, your family, friends, and the billions of people around the planet. It's not about you!*

With that, he realized he needed to fall in line with the conversation. "What do you mean? I thought my training was already advanced."

"We have been giving you specialized training for some time now, becoming more difficult as you progress. Let's say you have progressed to a level of 2 on a scale of 1 to 10. This is beyond what normal people can achieve. But you're not normal. Even the energy agrees. It said so itself. It said you haven't even begun to scratch the surface of how powerful you can become. But it also said that you're a battle strategist." Walter paused. "What do you think we should do?"

He's right, Zax thought. *I've always been smart battle-wise. Like when I tricked the D.M. into thinking that I was defenseless when, in fact, I had another weapon behind me.*

Zax folded his arms across his chest. "Didn't the energy indicate that Dax had been mistaken as a devil or demon in some cases in the past? Could that be or have been a religious belief? Maybe we can trace the origins of any religion that thought there was some sort of dark-powered evil or something like that. What if we research that aspect while I train to get past the surface of my power? If we find anything, it could be very useful."

Walter thought for a moment, pondering what Zax had suggested. "That's a really good idea. I'll start assembling a team of historians as soon as possible to begin researching religions."

Zax nodded. "Um, not to change the subject from this very important world-threatening problem that we are going through right now, but I have a question."

9

With all that had just happened, Walter could not imagine that Zax had something on his mind other than this crisis. Curiously, he said, "Sure. What's up?"

"Until all of this came up, I was wondering what I would have to do to work at The Office after I graduate high school. I mean, full-time, as a paid employee. I'd really like to work here and possibly have a career with the agency."

"With all of the specialized training you are receiving, and considering your special skills, I think you'd be a perfect fit as a permanent member of our organization," Walter said. "Typically, you have to pass several types of physical, mental, and academic tests as well as a background check and have an interview with the director. If he ok's you to work here, you simply fill out all the necessary paperwork and take an oath to protect our world to the best of your ability. Most agents are required to have a college degree and specialized training. You already meet many of these requirements, and some of the others might get waived because of who you are."

"Isn't Director Alvin about to retire soon? Is he going to make you the new director?" Zax asked. "Besides being his son, you have the best scores in…well, everything that is required to be an agent and a leader here."

"Thanks for saying that, but I don't know if I will be the one to take his place. Until he retires, he has the final say on every decision."

Zax put his hands on his hips and looked down at his feet. "I don't know why but he still seems to have a grudge against me. It couldn't be about what happened last year. I mean, that was over one of his agents who almost killed himself, trying to kill me." He lifted his head and looked at Walter. "You've got to admit; I did make a good point."

"It's not that. Truthfully, he's happy. He just feels bad—"

"What do you mean he's happy? He certainly doesn't act like it."

"He feels bad that he tried to stop you from saving Jaiden last year at the castle. He was being too protective and cautious about your power and thought you would get out of control if you used too much. He did the same thing with my mother. He was too cautious with what could happen."

Walter paused for a second, then continued. "Several years ago, there was a terrorist attack in a mall, and my mom—who was an agent at the time—was in charge of the team assigned to take them down. Dad was working with her. Somehow the terrorists were able to trap her and then use her as a shield. Dad had a shot at the leader who was holding her. He knew if he didn't take it, everyone in the mall would die. It was either her life or the lives of many. So, he made the hard decision and took the shot. The bullet went straight through her heart and into the head of the terrorist leading the attack. She died immediately; he didn't even try to see if there was another option. He just reacted and immediately killed her."

Zax did not know what to say. *Wow...he thought.* "I'm so sorry, Walter. I just assumed your parents were divorced since I'd never heard any mention of the director's wife."

"Yeah, it's a touchy subject," Walter said, wondering why he'd shared the story.

Zax looked up and stared across the catwalk at Director Alvin's office door. *I wonder what was going through his head while all that was happening?*

Dennis Eaves

Chapter3
The Third Basement

Dennis Eaves

42

Part 10

Zax left The Office and went straight home. Though his talk with Walter about the possibility of permanently working for The Office had been a brief distraction, his ride home was consumed with the immediate threat of having to face Dax. Likely sooner than later. It was not something he looked forward to sharing with Jenny, Ethan, or anyone.

Ethan and Jenny were snacking on popcorn when Zax stepped inside the house. Their eyes were glued to the television; NCIS was on, and he knew what that meant—nothing else mattered until it was over. Personally, he thought the show was overrated. But for some reason, they loved it. And somehow, they always solved the murder correctly before who did it and why, was revealed.

It appeared the program was in its final stages, so Zax decided to use this time to think about how to explain this new, dangerous, life-threatening challenge to his parents.

"Hey," Zax said as he walked behind their recliners to the kitchen. "Any left?"

"Yeah," Jenny said without taking her eyes off the television. "On the counter."

From the kitchen, he heard Ethan yell, "No…it was the store clerk!"

Zax rolled his eyes. He grabbed a bowl from the cabinet and filled it with the remaining popcorn. He heated it in the microwave for fifteen seconds to warm it up and sat down at the kitchen table.

Why are they so obsessed with this show? he wondered, as he had so many times. *And why am I eating this stale popcorn?*

By the time he had emptied his bowl, NCIS was over. He put the bowl in the dishwasher and threw his napkin in the trash. He went into the living room, where Ethan was still gloating about correctly solving the murder before Jenny. He hated to disrupt Ethan's moment of joy, but he had to tell them what he had learned at The Office. And he had to do it now.

He walked around Jenny's chair and sat down on the sofa. After a heavy sigh, he told them everything.

11

When Zax finished talking, the room went silent. The only sound they heard was the rapid beating of their own heart. The harshness of what he said horrified them. After hearing that the world might end, they were terrified not only for him and themselves but for everything and everyone.

"So, you're going to have to battle against a demon?" Jenny asked with a soft tremble in her voice.

"Yes and no," Zax said calmly. "Dax isn't a demon. But according to the energy, he is mistaken as one. And because of that, we're going to look into different religions and see if any of them can provide any information as to how to defeat him, or anything at all about this situation. Hidden in the archives might be clues that would help explain why the energy is here and what its purpose is."

"But there are so many religions and so much data. How are you going to know which one is the right one?" Ethan asked skeptically.

"I have a theory, but I need additional information to confirm several assumptions."

Just then, both Jenny and Ethan's phones dinged. Jenny grabbed hers off the coffee table; Ethan pulled his from his pocket. After reading the text, Jenny sighed. "Well, I guess everything you told us explains this order from The Office," she said.

"What order?"

"To unlock the third training basement," Ethan said, still looking at his phone. "All the training you have done, which everyone in The Office does on the daily, isn't enough for you anymore. A few months ago, The Office developed a new training area, specifically and solely for you."

"We weren't sure if you would need to get any stronger," Jenny said. "We thought Professor Brian was going to be the worst of everything and that his premonition about Dax wasn't real. That it was just to intimidate you, so we kept it quiet. It turns out we were wrong."

"What kind of training? And when did we get a third basement?"

"To be honest, we don't know what kind of training it will be," Ethan said. "Remember when you were at summer camp, and we were gone to take down the Mexican cartel?"

Zax nodded; he remembered that time well. While he was having fun, they were risking their lives. He never understood why The Office hadn't sent him on that mission—or any mission of that nature—knowing his powers.

"When we got back, Jenny and I were told about the basement. Apparently, it had been a part of the original house design; we just didn't know it. While we were gone, The Office sent some construction workers over to create an access and a scientist to set it up. They pulled out all the stops and completed the work while we were away. They told us not to mention it to you. I think they hoped that we'd never need to use it."

Their phones dinged again—this time with an access code allowing entry into the previously prohibited room.

"Looks like it's time to find out what's inside." Jenny turned her phone towards Zax, showing him a series of numbers.

The three of them headed to the elevator which led to each basement level—the simulator room, the gun range, and now, the new special training floor. When the doors closed, Ethan entered the new 12-digit code from The Office text, and the elevator began to move. Once the elevator got to the new third-level basement, Ethan entered a second 12-digit identification code from The Office text, and a security lock clicked. The elevator doors parted.

12

They stood still for a moment, taken aback by what they saw. Or, more appropriately, what they didn't see. The room was pitch black, yet in the far distance, they were able to see the opposite wall—barely. Based on their limited visibility of the wall, all they could tell was that the room was large. And that they could see nothing else.

Ethan took Jenny's hand and cautiously led her into the darkness. There was nothing in the room as far as they could tell; nothing but a haunting, eerie silence. They instructed Zax to stay in the doorway until they checked it out, but when he could no longer see them, he stepped into the room.

Instantly, the entire room was flooded with bright, white fluorescent lights and a loud robotic voice blared, "Energy Signature Detected."

In the glaring light, they could now see a massive sliding door on the other side of the room. Within seconds, the door opened, and a giant, lanky, remarkably familiar lizard appeared. It was the Chupacabra, a beast Zax had slain. It was on the other side of the room, but it didn't move. It just stood there, still, like a statue.

"What the hell? What kind of training is this? How is the Chupacabra here…I killed it last year!"

Ethan turned around and caught sight of what looked like a panel on the wall next to the elevator door. Hurrying to it, he saw a button labeled "Tutorial." As soon as he reached the panel, he pressed the button, and the Chupacabra went back into the room from which it came. The colossal door closed, securing the beast behind it. Simultaneously, an imposing hologram of a scientist in a white robe with frizzled hair and frameless glasses appeared.

"Hello Zax. Welcome to the special training room," the mysterious hologram said. "My name is Dr. Reeves. I am the scientist that office agents contacted to research the ooze from Professor Brian's castle and determine what it was. Once I analyzed it, I realized something was missing from the formula he'd used to make the first three beasts. So, I tracked the purple dust in the atmosphere that the creatures had left behind after you killed them and analyzed it. When I did, I noticed something astonishing. It was like every dust particle was its own lifeform, a bunch of microorganisms that take control and enhance their host.

"After that, I gathered some dead lizards and put a few dust particles in the mixture of the ooze. This way, these lifeforms could take complete control of their host without fighting with the white blood cells, T-blood cells, and other defenses inside the living lizard that Professor Brian used. The combination started to bubble and began to grow and grow and grow. Finally, it took the form of the Chupacabra, like the beast you once battled.

"I added some other chemicals to the mix to make the Chupacabra obey specific shock patterns. The shock patterns correspond with the buttons on the panel by the elevator. The panel also has a detachable remote control. It functions the same; it's just portable. When the remote is detached, the panel can no longer be used to control the beasts—only the remote.

"No worries, it doesn't hurt the beast. When the buttons are pushed, a slight shock commands the Chupacabra to attack, turn around, lay down, or follow any other command. That is how the Chupacabra you saw earlier left, without hesitation, when Ethan interacted with the panel.

"There are also replicas of the Brute and D.M. For obvious reasons, we didn't let the D.M. have all its powers, like the hypnotic screech. Remember, the beasts in this training room are still just as real and still just as powerful, if not more, than when you fought them last. Good luck."

The hologram disappeared, and the massive door opened again. The device on the wall now displayed additional buttons—Chupacabra, Brute, D.M., and the numbers one through ten.

"This is way too dangerous. What if the beasts get out!" Zax exclaimed.

"That's why we have the shock learning feature," Ethan said. "Hey Zax, I'm sorry, but Jenny and I must go."

Jenny's heart raced; she was tormented knowing what Zax was about to face. She took a final glimpse at him and then ran to Ethan's side. *Please be safe,* she thought.

Zax stood still, staring at them, confused. He watched as Ethan pressed the Chupacabra button, followed by the circular button labeled "5" on the panel, then snatched the detachable remote off the wall. Ethan grabbed Jenny's arm and pulled her into the elevator. The door closed, and the elevator ascended to an observation deck that overlooked the room below—the room where they'd left Zax. Through the thick, glass-paneled wall, they could see everything. And as long as Ethan had the remote, he had total control.

The door on the opposite wall of the gigantic room opened, and the Chupacabra reentered. By this time, Zax realized what they were doing. His advanced training had begun.

He heard a thunderous grumble and quickly spun around. Four more Chupacabras burst through the door. And he knew who had unleashed the beasts from hiding.

"ETHAN!!"

13

The Chupacabras flew towards Zax at warp speed. Without a second to spare, Zax created a perfect spherical barrier of energy that encased his entire body. The torrential force of the Chupacabras hitting him at once sent him flying towards the wall adjacent to the observation room. Even though his body never made contact, the energy barrier did, and upon impact, small fragments of concrete from the cinder block wall crumbled to the floor and left a perfectly round dent in the wall.

Zax knew the weakness of the Chupacabra was right between its eyes, the only place on its body where its thick crocodile hide did not cover. He created an energy spear and threw it directly at the beast leading the pack. It hit the spot between the eyes of the Chupacabra, and Zax had a small celebration in his head.

Stronger than the original? Are you sure about that! he thought, laughing to himself. But then, to his surprise, the spear bounced off the beast. He had hit his intended target dead-on, but these beasts had been modified. They were now completely covered with a thick hide. There was no weak spot.

Stunned, Zax stood staring at the beast, who was still rushing toward him at full force. From the control room, Ethan and Jenny could see his confusion. They pounded on the glass window to get his attention, hoping to snap him out of his stupor. It worked. He glanced down at his hand and formed another spear to hurl at the approaching Chupacabra. It bounced off again.

No sooner than the weapon had flown from his hand, a second Chupacabra came from behind and tackled him with his snout, scraping him against the concrete floor. The beast then unexpectedly backed away, and Zax quickly got back to his feet. He wondered if this was how Jack felt when he used to get tackled playing football.

Disoriented thoughts were running a hundred miles per hour through his head as he looked around the room, trying to figure out how to defeat the enhanced beasts. He wondered how, or if, he could beat the five Chupacabras circling around. He had successfully taken one out last year, but that one had a weakness. Now there were five. Five with no weakness. Five with an impenetrable hide that covered every inch of their bodies and ricocheted all his spears.

He had to think of something to defend himself. And very quickly. He knew a sword or scythe wouldn't take them out if the spear didn't. Like the spear, they'd just bounce off too.

This left him with only one choice. He had to use the second-grade weapons—the ones he possessed while in the aura state.

He closed his eyes and tried to concentrate on something infuriating, like how Ethan had thrown him into this situation without warning. He knew that anger would make his energy gather and build up faster than anything. But right before the energy he'd amassed exploded into an uncontrollable blast, he realized why Ethan had done what he did. As this realization overtook his anger, the buildup of energy slowed. He knew Ethan had only done this to prepare him for situations like this, like the ones he would invariably be thrown into. Situations where you don't have all the information you need, but you have no choice other than to fight and win.

Understanding the reasoning behind Ethan's maneuver, the energy started to wrap around him and transform him into the aura state. He made the double-headed spear—the deluxe spear—and threw it at one of the beasts. The speed of the weapon traveled faster than any he'd ever thrown, and it pierced the body of one of the Chupacabra. The beast crashed to the ground. Upon impact, its form became misshapen before it turned back into the original ooze that Dr. Reeves had used to modify the beasts.

As he took his stance to take on the next beast, three of the remaining beasts melted right in front of him, creating four piles of ooze in the room. Only the original beast remained. Zax looked around, surprised. Not so much by what happened to the creature he initially hit but by the other three beasts that the spear did not touch. The spear had simply passed by those beasts, and the pressure emitted from the spear as it passed them was so powerful that it destroyed them, turning them into ooze as well.

From all his training, Zax's power had grown to new heights that even he didn't comprehend. Not his physical body, but his energy power. Through the training he had received soon after battling Professor Brian, he learned that his breathing, heart rate, and blood pressure all played a factor in his power. The more powerful the heartbeat, the more influential the energy, but the faster the heartbeat, the less control he had over the power. Since this discovery, The Office had him do underwater training and many other breathing exercises, including running at high altitudes while using a training mask.

Once he realized how powerful his energy was in the aura state, he thrust it across his arm, much like he had done at his old house when he first encountered The Office agents and threw them into the pond. The energy rushed towards the last beast and slammed it across the room and against the back wall. Upon impact, it, too, turned into the purple ooze.

14

When the last Chupacabra had transformed from its monstrous shape into a pile of ooze, sprinkler heads popped up from the floor and washed the remnants of the beasts away into the drainage ring lining the perimeter of the room. Once the ooze was gone and the sprinkler had deactivated, Ethan and Jenny came down from the observation deck back to the training room.

"I'm sorry for leaving you here without much warning," Ethan said. "But I knew how powerful you'd become and that you could take them on. Your power is going to exponentially increase with this training."

"It's ok, I understand," Zax said with a slight smile on his face. "I know you're not dumb enough to think you can kill me off that way."

Ethan was relieved that Zax understood. He patted Zax on the back, and they all laughed, albeit nervously, for a moment.

"How about we go get something to eat?" Jenny asked.

"Sounds great to me. I'm starving. Being in the aura state takes a lot out of me."

Riding up to the main floor, the aroma of lasagna began to tickle their senses. Jenny had put it in the oven just prior to NCIS. With the elevator door partially open, she could see across the room that seven seconds remained on the two-hour timer.

"Perfect timing," she said.

She picked up a couple of potholders to remove the hot Stouffer's lasagna from the oven and placed it on the stovetop. They loved lasagna, just not hers. And she wasn't bothered in the slightest.

Zax grabbed a bottle of water from the refrigerator and sat down at the kitchen table next to Ethan while Jenny served dinner. After two servings, he excused himself to go to his room. But before he left the kitchen, he tried to sneak some frozen yogurt for dessert.

"Saw that," Jenny said, grinning.

"I know," he said with a spoonful of yogurt in his mouth. "You always do."

On his way up the stairs, Zax began to feel a strange sensation, something more like a presence. A presence that didn't belong, especially while he was eating his creamy yogurt.

15

The NASA satellite sent to examine other portions of the galaxy—now a vessel controlled by an evil power known as Dax—was starting to enter the atmosphere of the Earth. Based on The Office's research, they had learned the point of impact would be an island in the middle of the Pacific Ocean; more specifically, the castle on the island where Zax fought Professor Brian and saved Jaiden, just last year. The island had been deserted since their battle. Though a plan had originally been devised to send agents to the castle to analyze the situation, the mission had been scrapped. Based on the warning given to Walter at office headquarters by the energy that had overtaken Zax's body, the potential loss of agents was not a risk worth taking.

The satellite rushed towards the remote island at extraordinary speed, traveling faster and faster, picking up more speed as it fell to Earth before it viciously crashed into the castle. On impact, the castle collapsed onto itself. It crumbled into pieces of stones that blasted away from the satellite. But as the stones flew, a single brick came tumbling straight down. It should have hit the satellite, but it didn't.

The brick landed on what seemed to be an invisible barrier made of Dax's energy and slid down the side of the barrier to the ground—just like Zax's energy had predicted. The satellite was unharmed. The pressure of Dax's power was so great that anything, real or perceived to be a threat to him, was blocked.

Strange purple-looking energy started to emit off the satellite, trying to take a human-looking form. But as it took shape, it ended up looking more like a stick figure drawn by a kindergartener than a human.

"So Zax, this is the world you tried so hard to defend from my beasts?" the stick figure said. "No matter, you will never be able to stop me." It then disappeared into the ground, leaving no trace other than the giant crash site and a crumbled castle.

Dax found that he could easily travel through the crust of the Earth. He needed to hibernate and make his presence unnoticeable. The best place, the only place, had to be somewhere cold. Dax's senses ran through the crust as if the Earth were his body, allowing him to find the exact environment he needed. He had to get to the coldest place on the planet, the East Antarctic Plateau.

Once located, he rushed to the plateau as fast as he could to set up a base of operation, hibernate and let his power recharge. In order to keep himself and the satellite from being destroyed or burned up when he entered the

Earth's atmosphere, he was going to need a lot of his energy.

When he got to the plateau, he dug a hole that tunneled fifty yards beneath the plateau's surface. Immediately following, he carved out a giant sphere about half a mile in all directions under the hole. As he carved the sphere, Dax left platforms that spiraled down like a staircase to the halfway point. There, he created a crosswalk that spanned to the opposite wall. Halfway across that crosswalk, he made another one that extended wall-to-wall, going left and right. Together they formed a perfect cross. On the far side of the crosswalk, he carved another staircase to the bottom of the sphere where an oval cocoon-like pod lay.

Dax descended to the bottom of the sphere and entered the pod. Once inside, he fell into a hibernated state to recharge his power. But the icicles that formed as a result of his carvings—the ones hanging onto the sides, under the crosswalks, and the ceiling—began to transform. They started to be affected by his power. They began to develop a conscience. Filled only with hate and despair, they broke away and left the base looking to wreak panic and mayhem out in the world.

Chapter 4
The Glaze

Part 16

Zax had trained the past couple of weeks in the third-level basement and had become better and stronger every time. In the beginning, he struggled to take on five Chupacabra, three Brutes, and two D.M.s— each type of beast by itself. But as it now stood, he could take on eight Chupacabra, six Brutes, and five D.M.s, all at the same time.

Although he was getting stronger, training harder, and becoming more prepared to take on Dax, Jaiden could not help but worry about his situation. On the night Dax landed—the night he and his parents had lasagna—Zax told her everything that was happening. The fact that something significantly more powerful than him might be hunting him was almost too much for her to deal with.

Not only that, but she also missed him. She missed not hanging out after school and the time they had together when he would drive her home. Since he'd started having to go straight home after school to train, she only saw him when they met after first period, in study hall, and at lunch. Seeing each other on weekends had become rare.

By the time Zax reached the edge of the parking lot to go back home to train, he could see Jaiden leaning up against his car. Her arms were crossed, and her backpack was at her feet. She had gotten out of class early to try and catch him before he left, which she did successfully. Even though he could not see her eyes behind her sunglasses, the look on her face told the tale. He knew she was upset about everything that was going on.

"I don't like how we rarely spend time together anymore," she abruptly said as he approached.

"I understand. I don't like it either. But if I don't become a lot stronger, I won't be able to defeat Dax."

"I know," she said. She stepped away from the car and gave him a hug. "I just miss you sometimes."

"I know, and I miss you too."

Then, without thinking, he pulled away from the hug and grabbed her hands. On an impulse, he said, "Hey, what if you come and watch me train?"

"Seriously? I mean, yeah! I'd have to ask my parents, but I don't think they will mind. They pretty much let me do whatever I want. Besides, they really, really like you." She grinned. "Almost as much as I do. They talk about you all the time and are always asking how you're doing."

Maybe I should have cleared this with Ethan and Jenny first, he thought. *Too late now!* Zax smiled and opened the passenger door.

"Why didn't we think of this sooner," she said as she hopped in and buckled up.

The smile on Zax's face broadened as he walked around to the driver's side of the car. "If they say it's ok, I'll take you home with me and bring you back later. Hopefully, they'll let you. But if not, I'll just leave after dropping you off."

"Oh, they'll say it's ok. Trust me."

17

On their way to Jaiden's house, they drove past the local Ace Hardware, Dollar General, McDonald's, and Subway. Zax could not help but maintain his smile as she talked non-stop about random things, jumping from one subject to another—everything from schoolwork to his training to some short stories she was working on in her spare time. *Clearly, she's excited. I hope they let her go.*

Zax had hardly pulled into her driveway before she bounced out of the car. "Wait here. I'll be right back," she said, running towards her front door.

"Okay," he said, knowing she had not heard him. He shook his head and laughed. But he was excited too. It truly had been quite a while since he'd spent time with her.

He could see a silhouette of Jaiden talking to her parents through the living room window. The screen on the window made it a little challenging to make out who was who, but not impossible. About ten minutes later, he saw what he assumed to be her parents nod. She gave them a quick hug and rushed for the door. Running back to the car with a huge smile on her face, she gave him a thumbs up. She jumped back into the car, and they pulled out of her driveway and headed for his house.

Once they got to Zax's and went inside, they found Ethan and Jenny pacing the floor, both very distressed. The extreme worry that consumed their faces and body language told Zax that something big had just happened or was about to go down. But at the site of Jaiden, that changed. Catching their look of disbelief, Zax knew he should have asked as they quickly tried to muster a smile. The last thing they needed was for Jaiden to know what was going on; they knew how much she worried about him.

"Hey Jaiden, we didn't know you were coming," Ethan said, cutting his eyes to Zax.

"Oh, is it not ok for me to be here?" she asked, beginning to sense an awkwardness among them. "Zax invited me to come watch him train, and my parents said it was ok, but if this isn't a good time…"

She looked at Zax, then back at them.

"No, it's fine. I'll bring you to the observation deck," Jenny said. "Come on."

Ethan and Zax watched Jenny and Jaiden disappear into the elevator. A worried, burdened look returned to Ethan's face as soon as the door closed.

Before Zax had an opportunity to ask what was going on, Ethan spun around and looked him straight in the eyes.

"We need to talk about something that we're assuming has to do with Dax, but we'll have to do it after you train since you brought Jaiden here," he said, frustrated, turning away. "When you're finished training, Jenny and I will drop off Jaiden, and you will go straight to The Office!"

What the…? Zax thought, watching Ethan walk away. He had been moderately concerned when he came in the house and saw the look on their faces, but now, that concern had intensified to the point of worry; their fearful anxiety had transferred to him.

The further Ethan moved away, the more serious Zax became. *I will do whatever it takes to protect everyone. This is what I have been training for over the past weeks.*

Ethan pressed the call button on the elevator and waited for its return. When the doors parted, he got in and looked across the room, holding the door. Zax knew what this meant. He followed in Ethan's footsteps, and they quietly rode down to the third level.

Ethan dropped Zax off in the training room and grabbed the remote off the wall, allowing him to control the beasts. Ascending back to the observation deck, he could not help but worry about Zax. He knew that Zax's power was connected to his emotions, and based on what he had just told him, he was afraid that Zax might get riled up or nervous and accidentally destroy the entire house out of his own fear of having to fight Dax sooner than he thought.

Zax glanced over his shoulder through the observation room window at Ethan, Jenny, and Jaiden. He nodded; he was ready. Without delay, five of each of the beasts—the Chupacabra, the Brute, and the D.M.—charged at him. But he didn't move. He needed to test his reaction time to the beasts and how fast his reflexes had become, something he would have shared earlier if given a chance.

Jenny and Jaiden began to panic and bang on the window. Ethan was panicking too, but he knew Zax could not hear them over the movement of the beasts. They had no idea what he was doing or why he was standing still. Ethan took a deep breath and tried to calm himself. And them. Trusting Zax was their only option.

Before their eyes, Zax disappeared and reappeared behind the beasts so fast that their eyes couldn't keep up with him. They could not process what had just happened. All five of the Chupacabra, three of the Brutes, the arms of a fourth Brute, and three D.M.s turned into the purple ooze.

At the sight of the ooze, Zax transformed into the aura state, which he could now activate instantly rather than having to build up to. He turned around and created a broad sword. With a swinging sideswipe, the sword gave rise to a massive energy wave—at least ten times stronger than the one on the beach in his battle with the Brute. It traveled at the speed of sound, and breaking the sound barrier, it caused an explosive boom that cut the remaining beasts in half. Purple ooze, once again, covered the floor.

Jaiden, Ethan, and Jenny stood paralyzed in shock and amazement after witnessing Zax take out all the beasts in a matter of seconds. Seeing him in action, Ethan and Jenny felt slightly better about him going up against what they assumed was Dax. But Jaiden still had a sick feeling in her stomach about this whole thing. She saw Zax's face. He looked weary and upset. Anger rose inside her, and she wondered why it had to be him who saved the world.

Zax watched as the lights in the observation room shut off. His training was over for the day. Now he had to deal with The Office. Whatever that meant.

He waited for the elevator to return from dropping the others off on the main level. When it returned, he got inside. As it began to rise, he wondered how they would react when they saw him. Though he was a little more relaxed than when he went in, he was still tense. And a bit nervous.

When the door opened, Ethan was clapping. "Amazing job."

"That was unbelievable," Jenny added.

"Thanks," Zax said. "Sorry if I worried you. I cannot imagine what you thought when I didn't move, but I had to test my reaction time and reflexes."

"You certainly passed," Ethan said.

Jaiden did not say a thing. Zax reached out and gently took her hand, leading her to the front door. He explained that Jenny and Ethan would have to take her home because he had to get to The Office asap. After a big, long hug, he kissed her on the cheek and made a quick exit out the door.

18

"What's going on? Where is everyone?" Zax mumbled as he entered The Office. He was beginning to feel uneasy, especially as he remembered the look on Ethan and Jenny's faces when he and Jaiden had walked in their front door.

About that time, he heard a door to his left squeak open, and Walter appeared. "You need to come with me. I need to show you something," he said.

Walter turned and started back through the open door. Zax followed as he continued to walk and talk. "I sent everyone home early today. There's just so much to take in lately. We got a report that several towns somewhere south of Chile and Argentina were attacked and that there were casualties. Our intel says the casualties seem to have been caused by icepicks skewering the bodies. We scanned the bodies and found residue of Dax's power."

Zax stopped. "Wait. Are you telling me that Dax is some sort of icepick-wielding maniac or something?"

Walter turned around. "No, we don't think so. We found traces of what were probably ice shards in the wounds. The ice picks were literally made of ice."

"So, Dax is an ice beast? Wouldn't that be the craziest thing we've ever seen," Zax said facetiously, trying to visualize what an ice beast would look like. "Any survivors?"

"Yes, there were survivors. They say they saw 'ice people,' and they described them as normal-looking people with two exceptions. One, they were made of ice. Two, their arms and hands were sharp ice spikes, not human. We're calling these ice people 'The Glaze' because their arms resemble icicles. And, as you know, glaze is just another word for icicle.

"There is one other thing...according to the reports, there was more than one Glaze. We don't know an exact number, but there were definitely more than the survivors could count."

"So, Dax isn't an ice beast? Is this supposed to be his army?" Zax asked. "He's moving faster than I expected. Is there anything showing where they went after the attack?"

"Not anything that we found, but the survivors saw The Glaze go back into the ocean once the sun started rising. We sent some divers to investigate the water, and The Glaze were still there, watching and waiting, not far off the shore. They didn't attack our divers; they just stood there facing the shore like statues."

Zax thought for a moment before responding. "So, you think they only move during the night, and you want me to be there when they do?" he asked.

"Basically, yes. If these are connected to Dax, they might be able to shed some light on him. And if they are like any other beasts that were created by Dax's power, only you can defeat them."

"Ok, I'll leave as soon as possible. Is the jet ready?" Zax asked. "Wait. What about school?"

"We got the jet ready because we assumed you would want to go as soon as possible," Walter said. "As for school, we met with the administrators and had them sign an agreement stating that as long as you finish all your work and turn it in before the end of each six-week term, you will be fine. Of course, you have to sign it too."

Walter lifted his arm and looked at his watch. "Let's go to my office and get your signature on it. I'll have a courier send it over in the morning."

They walked down the hallway to Walter's office, and Zax signed the document. As Walter was putting a post-it note on it with instructions for delivery, he said, "One more thing. Before you leave, I need you to go home and tell Ethan and Jenny that you'll be out of town for an indeterminate amount of time. If they have questions, answer them, but come straight back here, and the jet will be ready to fly you down. I'm leaving now, so I'll see you when you get there."

"See you there," Zax said and turned to leave.

Walking to his car, he wondered what these mysterious ice men, The Glaze, were and if they could shed any light on Dax, like who he really was or how to defeat him.

Dennis Eaves

Chapter 5
True Strength

Part 19

Within an hour, Zax was on The Office jet heading to the town where The Glaze had attacked, the same town where they had stood frozen like statues in the water along the shore. Eighteen hours later, he arrived at the ransacked town, having had plenty of time to try and make sense of everything that was going on and come up with a strategy.

By the time he got there and began walking down the main street into town, the survivors had been evacuated, and the bodies of the victims had been removed. Empty buildings and a few trees were all that remained. In the shadows of the buildings, chunks of ice left by The Glaze, unseen by the sun, were still frozen solid. Tree limbs were weighted down with icicles. The stores and restaurants that lined the streets were too destroyed to differentiate one from another. The ruin and destruction of what he saw was unfathomable.

In the center of town was an untouched patch of grass, roughly an acre, where Office agents had set up base. Sidewalks and streets outlined the grassy area. No cement, no buildings, not even trash, touched a single blade of the lush green lawn.

The base consisted of a large canopy with four six-foot folding tables arranged in a u-shape underneath it. Different types of guns and other weapons that The Office thought might be needed to help hold back The Glaze were laid orderly across the tables. Walter and a couple of other agents stood on the north side of the tables, checking the weaponry to ensure they were ready for potential combat.

"Hey Walter," Zax said as he approached the table. "If The Glaze are just sitting there, why don't we simply smash them while they're not moving?"

"We already tried," Walter said, studying the weapon in his hand. "Some of our agents died, and we can't risk losing more. Several froze to death in the water from the extreme cold The Glaze put off with their bodies. Others were skewered when they got too close."

"But I don't need to go into the water to destroy them or even get near them. I could just throw an energy spear or something."

Walter laid the gun down and looked up at Zax. "We tried that too. We decided to shoot one from afar with a sniper rifle—and it did shatter—but then, what looked like a purple liquid came out of the broken ice and dissipated into the water before we could react. We don't know what effect it will have on the ocean, so we can't risk destroying them in the water and end up mutating some kind of fish monster," Walter explained. "And even if we could, trying to pull them out of the ocean would be a waste of time because there are just too many. It would be faster to wait until sundown and have them come to you."

Zax thought for a moment. What Walter said made sense and sounded reasonable.

"I agree," he said, looking out over the lawn. "Since we still have some daylight, I'm going to explore the town so that when the fight starts, I can have some knowledge of the battlefield and possibly have a little bit of an upper hand."

"Good idea. Just make sure you're back before dark. We need to be ready for them when they come on land."

"Will do," Zax said as he walked away across the grass to the sidewalk and headed towards town.

20

Zax roamed the streets of the town, looking carefully down the alleyways and behind buildings to see if there was anything he could use during his battle—a sewer system, a dumpster, anything. It suddenly became clear to him that everything he saw, given a bit of creativity along with his power, could be helpful in some way if applied correctly to the right strategy.

After walking for about half a mile, Zax stumbled into the section of town near the shore. A once prominent blue and gold banner that welcomed visitors to Ocean Park now dangled by one corner from a flickering streetlamp, flapping noisily in the wind. Beneath the sign, a three-foot flashing barrier covered in caution tape warned against getting any closer to the shoreline, which was one city block ahead. *I'm fighting these things. Why would this barricade be for me?*

He glanced at his watch and realized it was getting late. The sun would be going down soon, but he needed to know every inch of this place. *I'll make it back in time,* he thought, *but right now, I'm going in. If nothing catches my eye, I'll leave.*

Shifting the barrier to the side, he crossed the warning line. The air temperature immediately dropped by ten to fifteen degrees. The further he got away from the barricade, the colder it became. More and more ice spikes began appearing on the buildings and coming out into the streets. The sun was getting lower, faster than he expected, and was almost completely down. If he were to get back to Walter on time, he had to get moving.

21

As he approached the corner of First Avenue and Ocean Drive—the street he walked into town on and the street that paralleled the shoreline—to circle back to base, he abruptly stopped. He felt something. He did not know what it was, but he knew it was not something physical; it was more like a dark intuition, a bad feeling. And it was pulling him in its direction. Though he had little time to spare before sundown, he could not abandon whatever this was. He had no choice but to follow the tug and investigate. Picking up his pace, he began moving again.

Rounding the corner onto Ocean Drive, he found himself in some sort of a plaza that was filled with carnival rides, colorful vendor stands selling goods, and gazebos adorned with gaudy decorations. It was obvious this oceanside location had been the site of a festival. But as he looked closely across the plaza, he saw that this was no celebration. Covering the entire plaza was something he had never seen before in person, only in tv shows and movies. The Office agents had not prepared him for this, and he did not know how to react.

Lying directly ahead of him was a field of corpses with ice spikes coming out of their bodies. He felt as though he had slammed into an invisible wall and could not move forward. In a state of shock, he stood motionless and stared at the mass of bodies scattered about the plaza. Even in the frigid temperatures, the stench of rotting flesh filled the air.

Everywhere he looked, there were bodies. They were bent over their vendor stands; they were lying inside the gazebo; they were in the street. Young and old, boys and girls, rich and poor. All of them dead. The Glaze had been merciless. They had no morals. Their only objective was to create chaos in Dax's name. And they had succeeded.

Zax no longer cared if he made it back in time. He was overwhelmed at the magnitude of corpses piled up and overcome by a combination of anger and sadness. He was told there were casualties, but he didn't expect this many, and he certainly had not expected to stumble upon them. He thought they had all been removed. At this moment, he felt he was to blame for all the deaths. *I have the power to protect people who can't protect themselves. Can I really call myself a hero if I can't do what is literally my job description?*

The longer he stared at the carnage, the more he realized he was not the only one to blame. "I should have destroyed Dax before he landed on Earth! It's his fault for coming here in the first place!"

His emotions were getting out of control, causing energy to build up inside him. But this energy was different. It was not like his aura state where the energy embraced and flowed with him. This energy—generated by the anger inside his body—was too much to keep inside, and it began to pour out of him, much like a cup overflowing with water. Though not in the aura state, he had the same amount of strength as if he were. His training had equipped him to have maximum strength whether he was in that state or not. The only different thing the aura state could provide now was his ability of flight and second-grade weapons. Until he found another way to somehow break through his limits, this was the strongest he would ever be. And all it took was for him to snap.

22

The sun had disappeared, and darkness had set in. A few streetlamps that faded in and out and the moon were the only things providing light into the plaza and onto the streets.

The Glaze had started to march out of the ocean, glistening under the night sky. The sound of their feet thumping against the sand and asphalt sounded surprisingly like an ordinary human. As Zax watched them pack into Ocean Park, overwhelmed by their size, he failed to see that several dozen had inched past him. Once The Glaze realized that Zax had not noticed their passing, they turned and attempted to rush him from behind. But before they could reach him, they melted into puddles of water. They could not withstand the heat from his energy, caused by his rage, that emitted off his body.

Zax focused his attention on the mass casualties in front of him, and in a solemn tone, he spoke to the victims.

"I make this oath. I swear on all the people killed by the hand of Dax, I *will* kill Dax with my true power, and then, as he enters the afterlife, you may do what you please with his soul."

He had not even noticed The Glaze that had melted behind him.

23

own the shore, The Glaze were still rising from the ocean. The ones who escaped melting, advanced rapidly into town towards Walter and the agents. Much like he had expected, they could do nothing to stop them. Despite their best efforts, all they could do was momentarily stun them by shooting their heads, which regenerated quickly.

Where the hell is Zax? Walter thought. He was pissed off that Zax hadn't stuck to his command. He reloaded his gun and took another shot.

Back in the plaza, Zax watched The Glaze move further into town. He knew he had to get back and warn Walter of what was coming. Spying a manhole near the center of the plaza, he determined that this was the quickest way back—and the best way to avoid The Glaze. He lifted the cover and dropped down into the underground sewer system and followed the tunnels. As he ran through the maze, the energy seeping from his body earlier had gone away. Though he was still angry, he had calmed down enough to keep the energy contained. He was back to normal. Moments later, he emerged from a manhole to the left of The Office's command base.

"Where the hell were you!" Walter yelled angrily. "I told you to be back before sunset!"

Just then, one of The Glaze made its way around Walter. It raised its spiked arm and pointed it towards Walter's back. It was aiming for an attack.

The arm broke free from The Glaze's body and raced through the air. Zax saw what was happening and formed an energy spear straightaway. Hurling it with all his strength, the energy spear shattered The Glaze and the spike with only a split second to spare before it hit Walter.

Zax turned to Walter and looked at him with contempt. "Why the hell didn't you tell me there was a field of bodies in the plaza by the shore?! Mangled bodies were strewn everywhere with ice spikes poking out of their bodies! These were children, seniors, women, and men who didn't do anything wrong...all of them, folks who came into town and just wanted to have fun!"

"Crap," Walter said under his breath. "I didn't expect you to go that far."

He then looked Zax directly in the eyes. "I didn't want you to freak out and become unfocused. We need you to be on your 'A' game for the battle."

"I understand that. But I'm not a kid. I think I need to know about something like a pile of bodies! I mean, if the battle had led there, and I stumbled on the bodies without knowing about them, I would've had to deal with seeing them in the middle of the fight. Not to mention the bodies could have been further decimated in the crossfire!"

"I didn't think about that. I'm sorry. I promise I had the best intentions. I swear I did."

"I know." Zax looked down, thinking of all the corpses he saw back in the plaza and the possibility of how many more people might die if he didn't stop The Glaze here.

All of a sudden, he realized The Glaze had surrounded the base. Walter, Zax, and the other agents were trapped. The temperature dropped exponentially at the presence of their icy bodies, and everyone entrapped could see their breath as they exhaled into the brutally cold air.

Walter and Zax put their backs to each other.

"My bullets have no effect on these guys. The best they do is stun them for a few seconds. When they are out of the water, you're the only one who can permanently destroy them," Walter whispered.

"I've been wanting to try something, and I'm guessing now would be the perfect time," Zax said. "Here we go!"

He grabbed Walter's gun and infused the energy into the weapon. Over the last year, he'd learned to control his power enough to keep the gun from getting extremely hot—too hot for him to hold—as it had with Jaiden's phone or the director's gun. Zax tossed it back to Walter, who immediately tested the energy-infused gun on one of The Glaze that was getting ready to attack. When the bullet hit the ice beast in the head, it exploded on contact and did not regenerate like before.

Walter continued holding off their enemy while Zax made an energy sword. Then, with one swipe, he took out three of The Glaze at once. Some he cut in half horizontally, and some, after cutting off their arms or legs, he beheaded. With Walter's modified gun and Zax's sword, they took out each of The Glaze surrounding the base in a matter of minutes. The other agents, struggling with the unmodified weapons that simply slowed the enemy, had been of little help in the battle.

Zax put bubbles of energy around the remaining Glaze and then began to shrink the bubbles, smaller and smaller, until The Glaze were crushed into small particles of ice dust. The ice shards that fell to the ground were like the dust that appeared when Zax took out the first three beasts, unlike the strange purple liquid produced in the ocean. *These things didn't shed any light on Dax but coming here did make me hate him more than anything I've ever known,* he thought.

With a reprieve from The Glaze, the entire team of agents, along with Walter and Zax, hurried to the plaza to begin identifying the bodies so they could be returned to their families. Using the energy, Zax melted the ice spikes that pinned the bodies to the ground, and the daunting task began. Walter contacted Director Alvin, and he agreed, on behalf of The Office, to hold a large funeral in honor of all the people who had died.

24

On the day of the funeral, Zax couldn't stay away. He felt obligated to be there. The Office had set up a temporary stage in the middle of the plaza where the bodies had once laid. As crowds of people gathered to mourn, raindrops began to fall. But no one seemed affected by the sudden rain. They were there for a reason, and the weather was not a factor. They were there, huddled together, to honor all the victims.

Agent Hastings had been selected to read the names of the deceased. As he called out each name, family members made their way up the steps to the stage and shook Walter's hand. Walter told them that he, and The Office, were genuinely sorry for their loss. Thanking him, they continued across the stage and made their way back to their spot in the field of people.

Once all the families had been acknowledged, Agent Hastings said, "Now that we have paid respects to each person who was killed, we will send their bodies to the families who shall decide what to do. Be it cremation, burial, or whatever. The choice is yours. Again, please accept our deepest condolences."

Zax watched as the families and funeral-goers slowly began to leave. But as he stared across the stands at their grieving faces, all he could envision were the bodies he had stumbled upon—the ones that had been lying where they now stood. He remembered each body and where it had been; he remembered the stench in the air. And he could not let the mourners go without addressing them.

Shooting up to the stage, he grabbed the microphone from Agent Hastings. From this vantage point, he could see the entire plaza, and it took his breath. Every time he blinked or closed his eyes, he saw each body, what each one looked like, and how many there had been. As difficult as it was, he had to speak.

"Everyone, please wait where you are. My name is Zax, and I'm sorry I couldn't be here sooner to save the people who lost their lives. I promise that the person who sent The Glaze, the ice people, will be taken down so that he can't hurt anyone else. This is my oath to you and to the spirits of all the lives that were lost," Zax said with his eyes closed, not once opening.

"Zax," Walter said quietly under his breath.

The crowd silently parted, with only a few people stopping at the sound of Zax's voice. Most continued to walk away, not even bothering to hear what he had to say. *I don't blame them,* he thought. *They are in shock. No matter what I say, I can't bring their family or their loved ones back. They need to get home and grieve.*

The next thing he knew, those who stayed behind and heard what he said were coming up to him and telling him how grateful they were that he cared so much for their small town, about the people no one else cared about. Though there weren't many, there were enough to make him want to stay true to his word. No matter what.

25

Zax and Walter gathered their things and made sure everything was stable before they hailed a cab to drive them to their awaiting jet. They had to be back in the Tacoma office in three days to reassess their plan of attack and report face-to-face to the director. He insisted.

Other than the faint clicking of the taxi meter mounted on the dash and the moderate road noise, Zax, Walter, and the cabbie, rode in silence for the first few miles.

"I'm sorry," Walter said, looking out the left backseat window. "I should have told you about the casualties as soon as you arrived."

Yeah, you should have, Zax thought. Staring out his window, he watched business owners beginning to repair their damaged buildings. "It's fine," he said. "You had good intentions. I don't think I would have gotten to this new level of strength had I not seen the bodies the way I did. The only problem is that I think I'm at my max." He clenched his fist. "What if it's not enough to take down Dax? After I made that promise, what if I can't do it?"

"You will find a way. You always do," Walter said, turning his attention to Zax. "When you first learned about your powers, you were able to take down skilled agents of The Office. You did whatever it took to get Ethan, Jenny, and Jaiden out of your old house unharmed, even though you had never been in any kind of fight or had any training. And when you fought those beasts...they all had you pinned against a corner in one way or another, but you still found a way to defeat them and protect everyone around you. Even with Professor Brian, you found a way to defeat him and get back to the jet with Jaiden. Some people may see stubbornness or something like that, but that's not what I see. I see an extremely determined kid who wants to protect as many people as possible."

Zax didn't know what to feel. Though he appreciated the words of encouragement from Walter, he was not yet confident in himself. He could not let the townspeople down. Glancing over at Walter, he smiled uncertainly and then looked down at his lap. "I'm sorry too. I shouldn't have yelled at you."

"It's fine," Walter said and patted his shoulder. "It has been a while since someone yelled at me. I needed to be reminded that my choices do have unpredictable consequences."

They continued their ride to the jet without speaking another word. With the plane ready, they boarded and took off into the evening sky.

Chapter 6
History

Part 26

It had been several days since Zax fought against The Glaze in South America, and no one at The Office had heard any word from him since the funeral. This was their third day back; the day he and Walter had to meet with the director. But first, he was going to school.

He arrived at school too late to meet with Jack or Mark before classes. This time he had to park even further away than the last time he was late. He had barely slid into his seat when the tardy bell rang. *I'll catch them at lunch.*

The morning classes seemed to last forever, but finally, the lunch bell rang. Zax got to the cafeteria first and waited at the back of the lunch line until Jack showed up— Mark always brought his lunch from home—then they funneled into the line with the other ravished teenagers. Jack, as well as Mark and Jaiden, knew that Zax could not elaborate on his activities for The Office in public, so they talked randomly about their mornings while waiting for their usual order. Chicken sandwich, fries, and Mountain Dew for Zax; cheeseburger, onion rings, and Pepsi for Jack.

"See you later," Zax said. He grabbed his tray and took off to meet Jaiden. "Tell Mark I'll see him after we eat."

Jack nodded.

Zax and Jaiden ate in the same spot every day. The exact spot where she had first given him her phone to listen to music; the singular event that had activated his power. Jack and Mark ate in the same place every day as well, but theirs was on the other side of the noisy room so that Zax and Jaiden could have some space.

Zax sensed something different about Jaiden. She was fine during study hall, but as he got closer to where she was sitting at the lunch table, she seemed as if she wasn't all there, like she was spacing out, oblivious to everything around her. Not really paying attention to, or aware of, anything. Even him.

"Hey Jaiden!" he shouted, standing next to her. Had he spoken softly, he doubted she would have noticed him or heard him over the collective mumbling of the other kids.

"Will you keep your voice down, you idiot?" she said and punched his arm.

"Sorry, but it seemed like you were lost in your thoughts and didn't see me. I was afraid you wouldn't know I was here if I didn't yell."

Jaiden smiled and laughed at his dorkiness and motioned for him to sit down. It made him happy to see her smiling. He sat his lunch on the table and took a seat.

"So, what were you thinking about that put you in such a deep space of mind?" he asked, popping the tab on his soda.

"I was just thinking about everything that has happened in the past few weeks," she said as she laid her head on his shoulder. "With Dax and all. How you have some secret past that could answer a lot of questions."

"Like what?"

"Like how the energy ended up being in the core. How a ball of energy has a conscience and can make the same conscience into human form. How you and Dax are connected. How—"

"Hey, it's going to be ok," Zax said, interrupting her litany of concerns. He kissed the top of her head. "The Office has researchers looking into all of that. You don't have to worry about it. And as soon as they tell me, I'll tell you."

Jaiden lifted her head off his shoulder and looked into his reassuring eyes. He smiled, and she knew everything would be ok. His smiles always made her feel better. They made her feel safe and put comfort in her heart. This smile was no exception. She smiled back, and the same security she felt from his smile, he felt from hers.

"I promise I won't let Dax hurt anyone again—not him, not his beasts, not anyone he might be controlling. I'll stop anything connected to Dax before it can hurt anyone, especially you," he said, looking into her eyes. She looked down. He took her hands in his and held them tight.

His phone began to buzz, crushing their moment. It was a text from Walter. The researchers had found something tying Zax and Dax to a religion.

"It's Walter. I've got to go. It might answer some of our questions," he said and hurriedly began to gather his things.

"Oh yeah, there's one other thing. There's something I've been wanting to test out. Once you get out of school, send me a text, and I'll text you the details. Can't tell you any more than that, but you will know what it is when I do it," he grinned.

As he jumped up to rush away, she grabbed his arm and pulled him close. "I have to pay you back before you leave," she whispered and gave him a kiss. "Please be safe."

Zax bolted out the door closest to the parking lot. He ran to his car, maneuvered it through the maze of parked vehicles, and headed straight to The Office.

27

Once he got to The Office, Zax sprinted to the computer lab where Walter's text had directed him to go, along with the directions leading to the room. Inside the room, several people were standing around in white lab coats and glasses—some male, some female, some with long curly hair, some with short straight hair. He assumed they were the scientists that Walter had gathered to research the religions and to try and find out about Dax, like exactly who he was and how, if there was a way, to defeat him. Looking around, he spotted Walter standing next to one of the men near the front of the room.

"Zax, come," Walter said, noticing Zax had entered and motioned for him to come his way. Zax walked in the direction of the two men, passing a table covered in papers labeled "Classified."

"I'd like you to meet Dr. Citlali. He is the lead researcher for the team looking into all the religions and cultures that might be tied together with you and Dax."

The man next to Walter stood about five foot six, had brown eyes under his black horn-rimmed glasses, and long thick black hair that was pulled back into a braid. He appeared to be of Native American descent. "Nice to meet you," Zax said and extended his hand.

"Hello," Dr. Citlali said, shaking Zax's hand. "I have been the head of this research team and project for quite a while now and thought it was time to share some of our findings."

"So, is there anything that can help us defeat Dax? Or anything useful to us?" Zax asked.

"We don't know yet, but we have found some pretty interesting stuff about you and Dax," Dr. Citlali said. "We assume it is about you two, at least."

Walter pulled a screen down from the ceiling and turned on the projector that was sitting on a pedestal in the middle of the room. The image that popped onto the screen was a photograph of a hieroglyphic wall inside a temple—or something akin to a temple—of a person he deemed to be some sort of warrior. The six symmetrical blocks that formed the complete image, along with the unreadable symbols around those blocks, had led Zax to this deduction. Who or whatever it was, seemed familiar to him, but he couldn't put his finger on it.

"This is one of the Aztec gods, Huitzilopochtli. He was known as the Father of the Aztecs. The eagle is also a symbol for him, as is the sun. He had a rivalry with his sister, the goddess of the moon," Dr. Citlali said.

"And what does that have to do with Dax or me?"

"Well, I have a theory, but that's all that it is, a theory. I think that you are supposed to be Huitzilopochtli. But over many years, the stories were altered. Instead of tension between two beings of energy that seem to be at each other's throats, according to what the energy said when it took over your body, the different religion and culture changed it into a rivalry between a brother and a sister," he explained.

"Wait, you think this god is supposed to be me?" Zax asked, surprised.

"Yes. Primarily because of the rivalry. But also because of the sun symbol found on the temple major in the capital of the Aztec. The circular symbol appeared to have rays coming off it. I believe that is a symbol of the energy in the core, the energy that you control."

"Ok. I guess that makes sense," Zax said. "But what about Dax? If Huitzilopochtli had a rivalry with his sister, and if that's supposed to represent the battle between Dax and me, then shouldn't the sister tell us about Dax?"

"Not exactly. If the story changed so much over the years as to change his gender, then who knows what else has changed? Plus, we couldn't find that much information on her."

"Is there anything else?" Walter asked.

"Well, we've looked into a multitude of Mesopotamian religions, religions with multiple gods, and they all seemed to have something in common—that one god created something and had a conflict with another god. The Aztecs, though, had the only god who fit the description and had some hint of being connected to the energy," Dr. Citlali explained.

"What if one thing from each religion connects it all together?" Zax suggested. "Like an enormous puzzle."

"Could be," Dr. Citlali said, pausing to consider the possibility. "You know, another thing that racks my brain, though, is all the other gods that people came up with. For example, Greek mythology has a lot more than just two gods, and that's not even including the demigods. I thought it was just you and Dax. But could there be other people who have the same power as you two?"

"No. If there were, we would have gotten a similar reading to Zax and Dax when we did the scans. So far, we have only seen those two," Walter said.

"Ok. We'll keep looking and see if we can find other pieces of the puzzle," Dr. Citlali said and turned back to study the image on the screen.

"While you're doing that, Zax and I will brainstorm new ideas to take down Dax," Walter said. He looked at Zax and asked if he was ready to go. Zax nodded affirmatively.

As they reached the threshold to leave the room, Dr. Citlali shouted, "Wait! There is something else I remembered."

Walter and Zax abruptly turned around.

When Dr. Citlali was confident he had their undivided attention, he continued. "There was one word that kept showing up when we investigated these gods of creation. The word 'spark.' It was always in the culture's language, so I thought it was nothing at first. But your power controls the energy in the center of the Earth, and that energy tends to create sparks."

"Interesting," Walter said. "Keep pursuing that angle. In the meantime, Zax and I will try to come up with our own theories."

"And you should," Dr. Citlali said.

28

Zax and Walter left Dr. Citlali and the other scientists and went to the room containing the hologram table. They needed to formulate a plan. They kept coming up with theories based on The Glaze and other things they knew about Dax, which wasn't much.

"What if I infuse my energy into some cannons or tanks? Like I did with your gun. Maybe that would be enough," Zax suggested.

"And risk blowing off part of the Earth? I don't think anyone would be ok with that."

Zax's phone vibrated in his pocket. It was Jaiden. She had just gotten out of school and was ready for him to try out whatever he said he wanted to try.

"Give me a second. I hope this works," he texted back, noticing that Walter was consumed in thought.

He gently placed his phone on the table and closed his eyes. He tried to picture himself outside of his body, looking back at himself like an astral projection before sinking underneath the Earth's crust. He imagined all the veins of the energy traveling through the crust of the Earth and imagined himself inside of one of these veins, traveling at high speeds and then sprouting out of the ground where Jaiden was. It was as if he were there in front of her. He could see her and touch her. He imagined picking her up and blasting off into the sky as if he were in his aura mode, flying off through the clouds and among the birds. He landed on the front porch of her house and then imagined sinking back into the Earth before rushing back through the energy veins to the room in The Office, where he stood next to Walter.

Zax opened his eyes, and his phone started going crazy, buzzing like a fly, with texts from Jaiden explaining what had just happened.

"All of a sudden, something that looked like you, but made out of the energy, popped out of the ground, picked me up, flew off, landed at my house, and put me down!!!" she texted. *"Since when could you do that!"*

"I wasn't even sure if it would work. I'm happy it did, though. How was the ride?"

"Amazing. It was like any other flight I would take with you!"

"Good to hear. I'll call you once I get home from The Office. We're trying to come up with an idea to take out Dax that doesn't cause half of the Earth to be blown apart!" Zax pressed send right before silencing his phone and putting it in his pocket, intentionally messing with her. He grinned, knowing she would be going crazy to get some answers.

He looked over at Walter, who was still deeply engrossed in thought and had not noticed his experiment or his texts with Jaiden over the last several minutes.

"You good, Walter?" Zax asked.

"Oh…yeah," he replied, snapping out of his trance-like state. He picked up the papers beneath the hologram and started to rifle through them.

"Question for you," Zax said. "How come we haven't used the scanner to find Dax? If he hasn't shown up yet, then he's probably still trying to get his strength back. Now would be the perfect time to take him down."

"We've tried, but we haven't gotten anything," Walter said, still rummaging through the papers.

"That doesn't make sense. We could pick up the smallest amount of his power on the satellite, but now that he is probably stronger and has more power, we can't pick it up?" Zax asked, confused.

"Well, even the scanner has limitations. It can't scan the entire Earth at the same time. And it can only scan about a third of a mile down into the Earth, no further."

"What locations have we scanned?"

"We've scanned North America, Central America, South America, and a few other places. That's about it. It takes a while to do a scan and a lot of resources."

Zax was stumped. *None of this makes sense. We can't waste time trying to scan the entire world. How do we narrow it down?* Then, suddenly, it hit him. "Wait! The Glaze. I think they're helpful after all."

"What do you mean? How?"

"The Glaze attacked the southern region of South America, right?" Zax paused, and Walter nodded. "South of that is the Antarctic. The Glaze were probably made from ice that came from somewhere in the region that was tainted by Dax's power, wherever it is that he is hibernating. If we can find out exactly where that ice originated, we could scan the area and see if Dax is there."

"That won't work. We tried. We know where the ice came from, and we scanned portions of that territory, but nothing came up."

"What do you mean you know where the ice came from? Why wasn't I told? Shouldn't I be kept in the loop with everything that has to do with Dax?" he asked loudly, clearly upset. Before Walter had a chance to respond, Zax added, "Whatever. So where was it? Where did the ice come from?"

"The East Plateau, Antarctica," Walter said, crossing his arms and propping up against the table.

29

Zax stood silent for a moment and looked at the floor, trying to calm down. He knew he had to get refocused and past Walter's omission—be it intentional or not—regarding the ice's origin if they were to move forward. "So, how far down does the plateau reach?"

"More than a mile. Why?"

"You said the scanner can only scan down one-third of a mile. Just because you didn't see anything on the surface or slightly below doesn't mean he didn't dig down deeper. I mean, when he got here, he traveled through the ground. Who is to say he didn't dig down more than a mile?"

"We thought about that too. If he did, there should have been some residue of his energy left behind that the scanner would've picked up, but there wasn't. Keep in mind, the East Plateau is a huge place. We don't know where he could be, and it would take ages to find out exactly where he is."

"What if the residue faded over time? His energy is different from mine, and if he is trying to get energy back, then he probably sucked up any residue he left. So maybe it works differently," Zax said. "And as for where to look, does anyone live in that portion of Antarctica?"

"There are people who live in Antarctica, but not many live in the East Plateau."

"What if we get satellite imaging for the entire plateau surface? I know it's a huge area, but we have the technology to do it. There must be something that can be seen on the surface. A hole or something."

"Well, what if the hole is covered in snow? It's going to be hard to spot anything on a map," Walter countered.

"It's better than doing nothing. Once we have the map, can't our tech team run a program showing the differences between Antarctica before and after Dax arrived?" Zax asked, becoming more frustrated.

He was still upset about all the people who had died in the small town and was exceedingly worried because they had yet to do anything to try and stop Dax. He felt like they had just been sitting and waiting for Dax to show himself, and if they continued to wait, Dax could kill a lot more people, especially when he was fully recharged. Walter could see Zax's angst; it was written all over his face.

"Ok. First, we'll do a complete scan and gather imagery. A comparative program like that should be easy for our computer team to develop," Walter said. He reached out and put his hand on Zax's shoulder and reassuringly said, "I promise we'll find him. And when we do, we'll take him out."

Zax nodded. Wearily, he looked to his left, staring at nothing in particular, and softly said, "I know. I know we will."

Walter patted Zax's back, then grabbed some papers off the hologram desk and left the room. Zax stood silently for a moment, reflecting on everything he'd learned. With a heavy, heartful sigh, he started home.

When he got home, he told Jenny and Ethan about their plan before going to his room. And as he promised, he called Jaiden and told her everything about the Aztec theories and the Antarctic. They talked back and forth about it all—making theories of their own—and wondered what would show up, if anything did, on the scan.

Chapter 7
Dax's Presentation

Dennis Eaves

Part 30

Zax received a text from Walter at 6:00 a.m. the following morning with news that the satellite scan of the Antarctic East Plateau was back. Quickly throwing on his jeans, a purple t-shirt, and black and white sneakers, he hurried down the stairs and out the front door as quietly as possible, hoping not to wake Ethan and Jenny. On his way out, he saw Jenny's phone lying on the coffee table and sent her a quick text explaining what was going on and that he had to get to The Office asap. He pulled out of the driveway and headed there posthaste.

After keying in the security code and entering the building, he rushed into the elevator and up to the control room. The only people in the room were the computer tech team—comprised of five computer scientists—Walter and, surprisingly, Director Alvin. The scientists were sitting at The Office's main control panel, typing code, which was being displayed on the sixty-inch monitor directly in front of them. Walter and Director Alvin stood behind.

Everyone glanced up at the sound of Zax's approaching footsteps.

"Hey Zax, come over here," Walter said as he entered the room and waved him forward. "The image captured by the scan should be up any second now. I received a notification that it was about thirty minutes from being completed when I texted you."

Zax walked over to Walter and stopped on the opposite side of where the director was standing. He wasn't too happy to see Director Alvin and decided it wasn't necessary to speak. At least not first. But his attitude and displeasure were quickly noticed.

"I'm sorry, but I'm here to do my job," Director Alvin mumbled sarcastically, clearly directing the comment at Zax.

"I accept your apology, even though you didn't even bother to come to the funeral," Zax replied with the same sarcasm.

"Are you two still bent out of shape about that stupid fight?" Walter asked. He turned to his father. "It was over a year ago, Dad. And Zax had a good point when he said that you couldn't beat him if he didn't have control of his power. So, if you couldn't beat him when he *had* control, how could you possibly have taken him down if he lost it?"

Director Alvin stood stoic.

Walter sighed, then continued speaking to his dad. "I know you were worried that he could end up hurting more people if he lost control, the same way you were with the terrorists who had mom."

Walter then turned to Zax. "And Zax. All we were trying to do was protect people in the event you *did* lose control. You both had good reasons and good intentions. But now we have a common enemy, and we can't do anything about it if we are at each other's throats!"

"You're right, Walter. I'm sorry. And I'm sorry for what I said to you, Director. It was uncalled for. We need all the manpower we can get," Zax said.

Director Alvin nodded without saying a word, remaining focused on the monitor in front of them.

Walter shook his head and looked back at the monitor himself. *Unbelievable,* he thought.

A few moments later, a flashing red notification popped up on the monitor. The scan was complete. Martin Langston, the tech team's leader, pressed a button in the center of the control panel, and a vast, predominantly white image appeared on the screen.

"Our programmers worked all night developing a sophisticated program to identify the differences between the scan that just came in and the yearly scan we perform, which was about six months ago," Walter said.

The original image covering the entire monitor screen blipped and was replaced by a split screen. The current image was on the right, and the image from six months ago was on the left. Both images looked practically the same.

"Well, that's not a good sign," Director Alvin said with his typical negativity.

"We haven't run the program yet," Walter said, annoyed with his dad's attitude.

Without taking his eyes off the monitor, Martin pressed a series of buttons on the control panel. He had worked for The Office for twenty years and knew where—and what—every button controlled.

A yellow vertical line began to go across the screen slowly. Going from left to right, it slid over the image from six months ago, then on to the one that had just come in. Once the line had gone from one side to the other, crossing both images, another screen popped up with a loading bar that read, "Please Wait." Ten minutes later, or thereabouts, the bar had fully loaded.

Everyone present was anxious to see if this was going to work. Knowing there was a chance, albeit slight, that a mistake had been made in the untested program or that Zax could have been wrong, tension filled the air. Their feelings of uncertainty seemed to make the time come to a near standstill. This was their last hope to find Dax since no one had any other ideas.

The loading bar disappeared from the screen and was replaced by a full-screen image of the current Antarctic East Plateau scan. The screen zoomed in drastically, going faster and faster until it homed in on the middle of the image—slightly northwest of the Plateau. There were no signs of humans or domesticated creatures, no signs of wildlife or vegetation. But one difference was detected. It was the only difference between the previous and current scans, and it was significant. The program had found and circled an igloo in the middle of nowhere.

"This has to be it! That must be Dax's hideout," Zax said. His heart raced. "There is almost zero possibility that a human being could have gotten to this remote location since the last scan and built an igloo."

"If so, there must be a tunnel that leads down more than a third of a mile since the scanners didn't pick up anything," Walter said.

"Get the jet ready. Put in the coordinates of that structure and head there immediately," Director Alvin commanded.

Walter looked over at Zax. "Let's go take him down."

Zax nodded and grinned.

Walter turned and left the room. Zax followed close behind.

31

Walter and Zax entered the hangar where their jet was being prepped to take them to the igloo. A cargo plane sat to its right, typically housed in another hangar. A group of agents armed with automatic guns stood alongside a group of scientists near the cargo plane, waiting for their own departure. Director Alvin had hand-selected these men and women to accompany Walter and Zax, deeming them to be the best of the best. Some of them were the agents that raided Zax's old house that he threw into the pond. The agents' mission was to try and take down Dax or to help Zax in any way they could, while the mission of the scientists was to study Dax during and after any encounter to see if they could find any weaknesses. Should something connected to him show up and be a threat again, they hoped to be prepared.

Half an hour later, Walter and Zax settled into their seats; they had to get moving. They needed to arrive before anyone else and scout the terrain to check for traps or any alarm system Dax or his creatures, The Glaze, had set up. As such, Walter instructed the pilot of the cargo plane to delay departure for forty-five minutes.

When the plane's door closed, Zax pulled his phone out of his pocket and called Jaiden. He wanted to tell her what was going on. He also wanted to call Ethan and Jenny, but with limited time to talk, she was the priority, and he knew The Office would tell Ethan and Jenny everything.

"Are you sure you're ready to take on someone or, well, something whose relative strength is completely unknown?" Jaiden asked drowsily after hearing everything. Still in bed, she rolled onto her back and rubbed her eyes, trying to wake up and shake off her worry.

"I have to be. Until I can find another way to get stronger, this is the strongest I will ever be in terms of the energy. We know that Dax is still trying to regain his strength, or he would have already attacked. This is the perfect time because he's at his weakest."

"Just promise me you'll come back from all this in one piece."

"I promise." Walter nudged him. "Hey, I've got to go. Walter and I have to get to work."

"Ok, I love you," she said.

"I love you too," he said and hung up the phone.

"So, what's the plan?" Walter asked.

"I thought that maybe I could trap him in a bubble of my energy and use the broad deluxe quad star to try and take him out. I came up with a new move while I was training against the beasts in the basement, and I think it will work," Zax answered. "If I'm strong enough, it should just take one shot."

"It's better than no plan at all, I guess," Walter said and shrugged his shoulders.

"I'm not taking any chances, and I'm not going to hold anything back against him."

32

They started their final descent and landed about half a mile from the igloo. The location chosen for landing was an almost perfectly flat plateau with no dips or crevasses, and the weather was cold, breezy, and overcast. They felt that they could not land closer and risk setting off any traps that Dax may have put in place to alert him of their arrival or any plans he might have made to destroy their jet. They needed to protect themselves and the jet to get home safely.

"Let's do this," Walter said and smiled nervously at Zax.

"I'm ready."

They unbuckled their seatbelts and went to the back of the plane to change into their winter gear, designed for protection up to minus one hundred degrees. When the door to the jet opened and the stairs were lowered, they were ready to set off into the snowy, icy environment.

The Office had designed a customized winter version of Zax's original suit with boots and gloves for climbing up and down ice and a thicker bodysuit. His mask had been redesigned into a fur-trimmed hoodie that connected to the back collar of the bodysuit. It extended down to his face, far enough to cover his eyes, with the same see-through mesh as the original mask. Though Walter's suit provided equal protection, it was simply off the rack.

Bundled up and toting oversized backpacks, Zax and Walter trekked through the minus seventy-eight-degree temperature. But even with their new winter gear, they felt like they would turn into ice cubes. The frigid air, coupled with the breeze, almost made it unbearable.

By the time they reached the entrance of the igloo, they had been walking for over twenty minutes. Having not, to their knowledge, triggered any traps or alarms on their hike, they felt it was safe to enter.

As they were about to step inside the domed structure, they could see the cargo plane in the distance. Based on its location in the sky, they knew it would be a while before the team arrived. But they felt they needed to go ahead and go in. They did not know when Dax would get his strength back or what to expect when he did.

Once they entered the igloo, they discovered a tunnel about five feet wide that led straight down. It had no ladder or other visible means to descend into what they assumed to be Dax's lair. Zax sat his backpack on the ice floor next to the hole and removed a thick rope from a side pocket. After securing it in the frozen ground using a metal stake, he dropped the rope down the side of the icy tunnel.

"Why don't you just make an energy elevator or something?" Walter asked.

"Because I don't know if Dax can detect the energy when I'm using it this close to him. We want to be as stealthy as possible during our descent," Zax explained.

"Huh. I never thought about that," Walter said, watching Zax climb into the tunnel and grab onto the rope.

Zax was halfway down the rope when he signaled Walter that it was safe for him to follow and gave him the okay. Repelling down the rope, all Zax could see beneath him was more tunnel. Due to the pressure of the snow and ice on top of them, the deeper he got, the warmer the temperature became.

When he reached the end of the rope, he could see the first platform was still too far to jump down to, and the tunnel walls were too smooth and slick to climb down. So, using the spikes on the front of his boots to kick into the ice and the small but effective spikes on the palm of his new gloves—almost invisible to the human eye—he worked his way down. Walter had the same equipment but without the cool designs. Since this didn't require the use of any energy, Dax wouldn't be able to detect him.

Landing at the bottom of the tunnel, Zax found himself inside the lair that Dax had made when he first arrived—a giant sphere with a staircase leading halfway down to a catwalk that spanned across the sphere and led to more stairs on the other side, going further underground.

Looking down at the bottom of the spherical lair, he noticed some kind of pod made of ice and suddenly felt a dark energy emitting from it. It was the same dark energy he had felt when the satellite landed on Professor Brian's castle. *Dax must be inside there,* he thought and glanced at Walter, who had just made it down the ice tunnel. Walter nodded, and Zax started down the first staircase. Walter followed close behind.

As they made their way down the staircase, Zax and Walter could hear the other agents beginning to repel down the rope back at the entrance. They glanced up and saw Agent Smyth, the agent in charge, take the first leap. Seconds later, a loud thud rang through the sphere, and they stopped where they stood. Agent Smyth, reaching the end of the rope, had slipped and fallen down the tunnel. He missed the first step and landed on the cross-platform edge, barely hanging on.

Zax and Walter ran like hell down the staircase and across the catwalk and managed to pull him safely back onto the platform. Zax looked over the edge of the catwalk at the pod in the bottom of the lair, terrified that the loud thud from the agent's fall might have alerted Dax. The pod had not moved or shifted. The noise did not seem to disturb or awaken Dax. Zax told Walter and Agent Smyth to stay where they were and keep his team there.

Zax crept down the second staircase on the other side of the crosswalk and kept his eyes laser-focused on the pod that Dax was hibernating in. When he reached the bottom step of the lair, he slowly approached the pod and cautiously extended his hand to wipe away the fog on the ice. No one was inside. The pod was empty except for some of the same purple residue that had been left behind from the destruction of the three beasts and The Glaze. Only this residue was in its purest form, and its purity is what he felt earlier when he first saw the pod. He immediately knew what this meant.

"EVERYONE GET OUT OF HERE!!" Zax yelled up to Walter even though he knew there was no way they could get out in time.

He had to do something if anyone was going to survive. He quickly ran up the stairs while yelling for the others to form a group.

As he reached the others, Zax extended his arms and began to create an energy bubble in the palm of his hands. The bubble expanded until it encased everyone in the lair in one giant bubble, including himself. But just as the bubble sealed, the residue in the pod detected Zax's energy and ignited multiple purple explosions. The rigged explosions ripped through the ceiling of the lair and opened a hole out to the sky. But the hole was only open for a split second before it was covered again by debris from the subsequent explosion, then another and another.

Falling debris surrounded the bubble and tossed it violently from side to side. The explosions were so intense that each one felt like an earthquake and each one, stronger than the one before, nearly destroyed the protective bubble. When the explosions finally stopped after a minute and a half, everyone had settled to the bottom of the bubble. They were all safe. Some had bruises and cuts, but no one died or suffered any life-threatening injuries. That was all that mattered to Zax.

33

As the dust settled and Zax confirmed that no one was seriously injured, he looked through the bubble at the large amount of debris that had fallen on top of it, burying them in an icy tomb. The only way for him, Walter, and the team to escape was to clear the ice chunks and shards of ice that blocked their escape. Using his energy, Zax made the walls of the bubble contract and then expand back rapidly, like pressing a spring and watching it launch into the air when released. He crossed his arms in front of his chest, then pushed them back out quickly to blast the ice debris away from the bubble and form an exit path.

He immediately turned into his aura mode and flew out of the giant crater, leaving all the agents inside. He was now confident they weren't in any danger. As he flew up, his hood came off and uncovered his face. Going from the hot pressure of the lair to the sudden crisp cold air made him stagger, but he quickly regained his composure and continued to soar into the sky.

High above the lair, Zax hastily stopped when he found himself face to face with a man who appeared to be wearing a skin-tight purple suit covering everything except his pale hands, feet, and head. He was six feet tall with long black hair, a widow's peak, and what seemed like cold, dead purple eyes. But his eyes were merely a distraction. He had a large, satisfied, menacing grin spread across his face going from ear to ear.

"Who are you?" Zax demanded.

"So, you don't remember? Disappointing," the strange man said. "I mean, we were the first beings in this universe."

"What do you mean?" Zax asked, trying not to show fear. The truth was he knew exactly who was in front of him; he just didn't want to admit it, even though the "first beings" comment had thrown him off a bit.

"So, you don't even remember that," the manlike figure said. "Fine. I'll tell you everything. I'll start with my name. I believe you are already vaguely familiar with me. My name is Dax. Ring any bells?"

Zax looked at the man, or whatever it was in front of him, hoping the utter fear written all over his face was not detected. He didn't want to believe that this thing in front of him could have made the entire crater he was just standing in, something that even he couldn't do in his base form or without the help of his weapons.

"How about a demonstration," Dax said as he twirled around and faced The Office jet and cargo plane used to get there.

Dax's energy began racing towards his body, coming from the explosions he'd detonated inside the crater he had previously made. The immense force of the energy's wind blew past Zax, startled him, and sent his hair blowing all over the place.

Dax raised his right hand—curled in a fist—and the purple residue, his energy, started to compress into a ball; it hovered over the same hand he had raised into the air. He pushed his arm out with his hand open and his palm facing both aircraft. The ball shot out a beam of purple energy that went rushing toward the jet and cargo plane. With just one push of his hand, he obliterated both aircraft, leaving nothing but a raging inferno in their place.

"This is what true power is. It's an art. Pure destruction through total strength and no mercy," Dax said, looking at the burning planes.

Zax stared at the destruction in front of him. He watched as embers flew through the air and felt the heat from the blast. Without a doubt, he now realized just how strong Dax was.

"How come you got all of your power back but never attacked?" Zax asked.

"I don't have all my strength back," Dax responded, still looking at his handiwork. "I am truly impressed with how quickly you found me. I could sense your energy raging more than usual, and that's when I decided to leave my pod early."

Zax had to act; he had to try and take down Dax. He'd thought a lot about what he'd do when this moment came. And now it was here. It was time to put his plan into action.

"Don't you ever underestimate me or my power!" Zax screamed as he thrust his hands in Dax's direction, encasing him in a bubble. But Dax seemed unfazed by his encasement. It was as if he'd predicted it or just didn't care.

Zax's energy began pouring out of his body like it had when he saw the bodies in town that The Glaze had attacked. He quickly made the round handle of the quad scythe with the four broad sword blades and the deluxe spearheads on the end of each blade and created the deluxe broad quad star. Using a new move called the shooting star that he came up with while training in the basement with the beasts, the blades started to spin around the handle. When they did, he shot a giant, extremely powerful beam of energy from the star, rushing toward the bubble encasing Dax.

Right before it hit—a mere split second before—Zax removed the bubble that encased Dax, and the giant energy blast hit him directly with all his power. A giant smoke cloud surrounded his body, hiding him from Zax's view. Zax's energy started flying out of the cloud into the sky; it was going back into the cycle of being used—going into the sky and going back into the Earth in the form of lightning.

Other than Zax's heavy breathing from using too much power at once, there was complete silence. Zax slipped out of the aura mode due to his low energy level and settled clumsily to the ground since he could no longer fly.

"Is that all you got? You've become weak. Well, weaker, at least," Dax chuckled as the cloud dissipated.

As Zax could now see more of Dax, he realized that it wasn't a skin-tight suit he was wearing after all. It was his energy. Dax's body was made of nothing but energy compressed into the shape of a human body.

While Dax hovered in the sky, Zax could see the hole that took up one-third of Dax's lower left body. His left leg, left arm, and bottom left portion of his torso were missing. Zax knew definitively that this was Dax's energy.

Descending back to the ground, Dax's missing body parts grew back. He landed in about the same place that Zax had landed when he could no longer stay in the aura mode.

"Like I told you, I didn't get all my strength back. If I did, my entire body would look human. But if I am being honest, I do like this form better," Dax said. "What's happened to you? You used to be a lot stronger. Not stronger than me, of course, but stronger than you are now."

"How did you survive that? That took all my power," Zax said, still breathless.

"That was everything you had?" Dax asked. He seemed confused and looked shocked. "Wait, you aren't connected, are you?"

"What do you mean?"

"It is best I start at the beginning. The very beginning."

Zax knelt on the ground. After using most of his energy trying to take out Dax in the attack, he didn't even have the strength to stand. Dax used the energy surrounding him to pick Zax up and lift him until they were facing each other.

"This is going to take a while. I decided it would be better to bring you up to me instead of me bending over. Human forms are so unpractical. Hope you have some popcorn. Ready to learn how everything started? Including this world that you love so much?"

Immediately, Dax began to tell the story of them, their power, and why there was energy inside the core of the earth.

Chapter 8
The True Beginning

Dennis Eaves

Part 34

Long before any planet was created or formed, there were two beings. They did not know how they came to be; they just were, and they never questioned it. They never thought if there was a being higher than them. One of the beings represented creation, determination, and the protection of others. The other represented power, destruction, and manipulation. These beings had no definitive form; they were simply massive balls of energy. The energy of creation was a transparent yellow, while the energy of destruction was a dark purple.

Both energies had one goal—to try and make the perfect planet by combining the right amount of each other's power. They had no clue what the "perfect" planet was supposed to be, but they felt they would know when it was formed. Before they created their planet, the energies decided to invest equal parts of themselves into their new world. But no matter how much they tried, their product was never sustainable. Either the planet was too unstable due to the weakness of the foundation, or the life force was too powerful and would fall apart or turn into a ball of pure gas. It became apparent that the foundation had to be made by the purple energy since it had a more solid power. But if the planet were to have life, the life force had to be made by the yellow energy since it was able to promote sustainability, cooperation, and progress.

Realizing this, they began experimenting with using more purple than yellow, but each time the planet became desolate and couldn't withstand life. They tried doing exactly fifty-fifty of both powers, but the planet would become too fragile and fall apart, or it couldn't hold life.

After numerous failed attempts at creating the perfect planet, the purple energy came up with another idea.

"What if we used the majority of my power and ten or even one percent of yours?" it suggested.

"What? That doesn't make any sense," the yellow energy objected. "Using your energy at a little over seventy-five percent—or even fifty percent—leaves the planet lifeless!"

"Who says it's because of my power that the planet becomes lifeless? Maybe you're just too weak. Maybe the answer is to put more of my energy into it for it to have life."

"No, we've already decided to stay near fifty-fifty of our powers. We've tried using a much higher percentage of both our energies, and it didn't work."

"You're so greedy, needing to have fifty percent or more of your power in a planet that will fail; you don't even care if we succeed in making the perfect planet," the purple energy blasted. "My power is stronger than yours. All your power does is act like a glue!"

"I already said no. Besides, what if you're wrong? I know how you are. We've only been spending time with each other since the beginning of time! You will throw a fit and destroy the planets we've worked hard on, and then you'll be drained of your power. It will take at least a millennia for you to be fully recharged. What then?" the yellow energy argued back.

"Who cares if I destroy them? They're all failures anyway. If they aren't perfect, then they're just fodder."

"Failed or not, we still created them, and they are our responsibility even if they can't hold life or if they are simply giant balls of gas. The ones I hate to make are the ones that fall apart. Those are the ones where we put more of my power. Watching something I made fall apart, failed or not, still hurts me."

The purple energy was getting impatient and frustrated with the yellow energy's idea of failure. "I'll prove to you that my power is better than yours. I'll beat you in a fight, and from here on out, we will put ninety-nine percent of my power into the planets. My power is stronger and more powerful than yours, and I'm confident it will work the first time!"

"No, it won't," the yellow energy replied, trying to remain calm. "For two reasons. First, I know this won't work and will only waste our powers and time. Second, I strategize with battle smarts while you are just strong. You would be stupid to challenge me."

Tired and frustrated with the conversation, the yellow energy floated off in search of a new place to make the next planet.

The purple energy became furious and tried to strike the yellow being with a purple beam of its energy. But the yellow energy, knowing the purple energy like it did, knew this was coming. It moved upward, dodging the beam, then flashed behind the purple energy.

"I told you that I am battle smart," the yellow energy said, agitated. "You are so predictable."

With that, the yellow energy created its own explosion from its body. From the sheer force of the blast, the purple energy went flying, spinning as it flew through the expanse.

Once the purple energy restabilized itself, the battle was on. The purple energy shot a large, single purple beam of energy, twice the size of the yellow energy's spherical body, towards its perceived target. The yellow energy retaliated by shooting five separate smaller beams, each shooting a bit later than the other.

The first yellow beam hit the purple beam and slowed it down. The next one slowed it down even more, and the third beam stopped it from progressing altogether. This caused a momentary stalemate. Once the next two yellow energy beams hit, the combined force of all the yellow beams began to push the purple beam back toward the purple energy. But before the energy beam could reach the purple energy, the force of both beams going head-to-head caused an explosion so massive and furious that a gigantic hole was ripped in space. This would later be known as a "black hole."

The battle continued, with each energy trying to destroy the other. In one of the strikes, the yellow energy's beam was shot by the purple energy, which caused the yellow beam to cave in on itself. This collision made another rip in space, this time creating a "white hole."

The battle between creation and destruction lasted for eons, creating black and white holes all over space. Neither the yellow energy nor the purple energy ever landed a hit on the other. As time went on, the battles became so wearisome that the yellow energy considered forfeiting to the purple energy so they could go back to trying to make the perfect planet. But just as it was about to convince itself to surrender, it remembered what it represented. In addition to creation and protection, it represented determination. And because of that, forfeiting was not an option. Knowing that the purple energy was just too arrogant to give up, it was more determined than ever to take it down. It had devised a plan with no intention of losing. The yellow energy turned around as if retreating from the ongoing battle and running away from the purple energy.

"I thought you were a representation of determination, yet now you run. You coward!" said the purple energy, chasing it.

The yellow energy continued flying away without acknowledging the purple energy. In a moment of distraction, it accidentally bumped into a white hole near one of their failed planets that had turned into a ball of gas, and it simply bounced off. Before it could recover from the bounce, the purple energy had cornered it between the ball of gas and the white hole.

"So, you ran away and then got caught in a corner. Now you have no choice but to agree to my deal," the purple energy laughed. "Accept your loss, and we can move on, and I won't have to hurt you too bad."

"I will never give in to you or let you get what you want!"

"You aren't in any position to negotiate."

"Actually, I can do whatever I want because I have already won."

"You are so stubborn and naïve. Accept that you have lost!"

"Why would I accept defeat when I know I have won?"

"Why are you so confident that you have won?"

"Simple, you can't destroy me. Not only will you be by yourself, but it will be impossible for you to create any planet without my power."

"Don't be so sure," the purple energy said. It raised its hand and shot its largest blast yet.

But it was to no avail. The shot went straight through the yellow energy, and its pulsing energy body began to fade. The yellow energy speaking to the purple energy was a fake—a decoy—and the blast that the purple energy had just shot was sucked into the white hole.

As the purple energy inched away from the cloud, which appeared to be the yellow energy in confusion, the actual yellow energy came from the other side of the ball of gas.

"That proves my theory correct. Those white rips suck in your power instead of repelling it like everything else does. What were you saying earlier? That I should just give up?" the yellow energy mocked.

"I am stronger than you! I have no reason to surrender!" the purple energy yelled, though it was beginning to worry.

"Do you remember when we made this failed planet?"

"Yes, we put more of your power into it than mine. It had too much life force, and it overheated. What about it?"

"Well, these are the planets that I love to make, even if it is a failed one. Bursting with pure life, pulsing like a heartbeat…it resembles life."

"Who cares? It's still a failure," the purple energy snarked. "We are here to create the perfect planet, not continue to create all these failures that don't do anything but take up space!"

"Yes, but I can still control the energy I put inside it."

Instantly, a beam blasted out from the side of the gas ball and hit the purple energy directly, but only with enough force to push it, not destroy it. It was not as big as the one the purple energy had launched earlier at the fake, nor was it intended to be.

"That was a dirty trick!" The purple energy stumbled backward as the beam began to fade. "It's not like it matters, though. I can take a hit from little ol' you."

Before the energy beam dissipated completely, the purple energy was thrown into the white hole next to the ball of gas. Since the white hole was made by the yellow energy's beams crashing in on themselves from the clash with the purple energy beams, the white hole was effectively made from the yellow energy. So, instead of the purple energy bouncing off the white hole like anything else would have, it was drawn and sucked into the white hole and could not escape.

"You greedy bastard!" the purple energy screamed as it was sucked further and further inside. "Once I find a way out of here, I *will* kill you!"

It was finally trapped with no means of escape. Even its voice couldn't escape the containment of the white hole. The only things that remained in the universe were the yellow energy and all their failed planets. Without the purple energy, no more planets could be made. Having nothing to do, the yellow energy sat alone in empty space.

35

With all the failed planets in the distance and the lonely isolation, the yellow energy began to go into a state of hibernation. The light from its energy dimmed, and its body started to shrink in size. The energy in the debris from the planets that were still infused with purple energy continuously fell apart and were drawn to its hibernating state.

Atop the dormant ball of transparent energy, failed planets kept piling on top of one another, each adding more and more pressure to the mound. Heat from the energy and the pressure from fragments of past planets began to melt the rock in the center of the shell—which covered the energy—and created liquid magma.

The shell's surface was massive, imperfect, and predominately covered with craters. Varying sizes of planet fragments, some much larger than others, had fallen into piles and formed the giant pits while mounds of rock covered the dormant shell.

Giant ice clusters had drifted close to the shell and crashed into the side of these pits, melting from the heat of the energy and the heat of the gas ball that was near the energy's original hibernation. The ice clusters, combined with the craters, formed the oceans that covered most of the shell and filled in the massive pits.

Pillars of rock grew from the ground and were splashed upon by the newly formed ocean's waves. Without meaning to, the energy that was deep in the center of this shell, in deep slumber, seeped its energy through the magma and water into these pillars and gave them life, creating man. The water and soil from the rocks caused vegetation to grow on some of the pillars that had been infused with the yellow energy's energy and splashed by the oceans, making women.

Thus, the first civilization on Earth had begun. It was called Tlemoyotl, the Aztec word for spark, which was initially the name of this first human civilization.

The Tlemoyotl knew of the yellow energy, for the energy they were infused with held its memories. But as some people didn't believe in the story, they went off to make their own stories of how the world was created. As time passed, Tlemoyotl ultimately died out. People began to formulate their own cultures and religions.

Yet the purple energy needed to have his final laugh. It managed to pour out a small hair-thin stream of its energy. By making it so small that it slipped through the white hole, it traveled through space and the atmosphere of the Earth to infect the residents of the planet. It created the ultimate evil and caused people who make bad decisions to come into fruition.

Everyone born from the pillars was infected to some degree with the purple energy; some were infected with greater amounts of energy, others less. Those infected with the largest amounts of purple energy lost their minds and became what could only be described as beasts or even monsters. Those infected with purple energy equal to the yellow energy they were born with were most humanlike and had no powers. But those born and infected with only a slight trace of purple energy were confused as gods or demigods by those who were most like humans—the ones with no powers.

Zax now knew everything. Dax had told him the entire story of how the Earth came to be and why the energy now resided inside its core.

"How, you ask, do I know all of this?" Dax quizzed, getting closer to Zax, who was still being held up in the air by his energy. "Because I was the one trapped inside that white hole for billions of years. I am the purple energy, and you are the yellow energy. Well, you are part of it. You're actually just a separate piece of the yellow energy."

"That explains a lot, I guess," Zax said, keeping his head down. "But what do you mean by separated?"

"Oh, simple. I am all of the purple energy condensed into this one form. Every single drop of my energy is literally at my fingertips. You, however, are just a sliver of the energy that was infused into the body trapped inside the center of this planet, like the demigods from long ago. When we use our energy, its remnants are directed back to the pure source unless it can't find it directly. Then it will force its way through anything, traveling at the speed of light to get back to the source," Dax explained. "That's how we always had energy while making the planets and during our fight, oh so long ago."

"You know, that was a long story. I've been using a lot of my time lately trying to figure out how to call my energy back to me, or at least get it to strike the places of Earth that I want it to strike," Zax said as he lifted his head and looked up to the sky. "And that story gave me enough time to figure it out!"

Dax raised his head to the clear blue sky, curiously wondering why Zax had looked up. Then all of a sudden, ominous dark clouds started to appear, and snow began to fall. As soon as the first snowflake landed on Zax's suspended hand, a giant bolt of energy struck them both; it was a giant beam of the energy—in its raw condensed lightning form—and all from the shooting star move Zax had done earlier.

The purple energy holding Zax went away. He thought that the beam was going to be enough to take down Dax or at least mortally injure him. But once the smoke from the bolt had dissipated, Dax was still standing. And without a scratch.

"Like I told you, I have all of the power of the purple energy while you only have a portion," Dax said. He was starting to get frustrated again. He realized that Zax had the same battle smarts that the yellow energy had long ago. "I will give you time to become stronger. After all, I want a real fight when I kill you. Obviously, you are extremely weak."

Dax turned and flew off to who knew where, to do who knew what.

Zax watched as Dax disappeared into the clouds; he was furious. Furious with himself for still being too weak to keep people safe from Dax and furious with Dax for the chaos he brought. Anger began coursing through his body, as did the energy, and he screamed with all his might. The ground around him shifted and began to crack. When it did, giant ice shards burst out of the ground and shot into the sky.

36

By the time Zax calmed down, the ice shards were beginning to melt. Another cargo plane had arrived and was waiting to bring him, Walter and the other agents home. He slowly made his way over to where the plane had landed, where Walter and the other agents were waiting. He was completely back in control of his emotions when he reached the plane.

"How did they know we needed a ride?" Zax asked, pointing at the plane.

"We sent a distress signal after Dax suspended you in the air," Walter said. "So, what did he tell you?"

"I'll tell you on the plane. It's a long story," Zax said. "Let's go home."

Dennis Eaves

Chapter 9
The Plan

Part 37

By mid-flight on their way back home, Zax had told Walter everything that Dax had shared about their past. He explained how their battle had lasted for years, why the energy was in the core, and why cultures seemed to have partial knowledge about their past—and how all those things tied together. Though he was talking specifically to Walter, everyone onboard seemed to be listening to his every word.

"Wow, so you and Dax were the first living beings," Walter said, flabbergasted by the story. This was not what he had expected, not what anyone had expected.

"I suppose, I mean, is a giant ball of energy with a conscience a living being? And is there such a thing as just coming into existence without the help of another being?" Zax asked rhetorically.

Walter shrugged. He didn't know what to think.

"Anyway," Zax continued, "that doesn't matter at the moment. Right now, I need to become stronger and defeat Dax. The question is…how? I'm already at my limit, and he took my strongest attack as if it were nothing. From the looks of it, I need to become a whole lot stronger. A little stronger won't cut it."

"We'll find a way. You just have to push past your limits. Remember what Dax said. The energy you possess resembles determination. I know for a fact that you can beat him with time and harsher training," Walter encouraged. "Is there anything we haven't tried that you can think of?"

"I don't know…" Zax said as he closed his eyes and leaned his head against the headrest.

He had to think long and hard. The Office had gone to so many extremes to make his power as strong as they could get it. They'd made a hologram training room, a recharge room, and most recently, a room where he could fight the beasts as often as he wanted, as much as he wanted. With his eyes closed, he sat quietly, trying to come up with something, or anything, to help him move past his current strength.

A few minutes later, he had a random, crazy idea. He nudged Walter excitedly before realizing he was resting. Walter shifted in his seat.

"What about the cultures?" Zax asked. "Maybe the answer lies there. We've found so much indirect information about me and little to no information about Dax or how to defeat him. We've only found hints as to who he is. But what if there's something in those hints that can also tell us how I can break my limits and become stronger?"

"At this point, we need to explore every possibility," Walter said. He took his phone from his coat pocket and texted a message to Dr. Citlali asking him to search for anything, any hint, that would help Zax become stronger.

After confirming the text went through, Walter closed his eyes and fell into a deep sleep. And so did Zax.

38

When they arrived back at The Office, Zax knew the first thing he had to do was call Jaiden. He needed to let her know he was ok after seeing the numerous texts she had sent, each filled with more worry than the last. But more than telling her that he was all right, he needed to hear her voice. It always seemed to calm him, regardless of what he was feeling. He took his phone out of his jacket pocket and tapped her contact picture.

On the first ring, his hands began to shake. He thought he had himself together but realized how distressed he still was from his encounter with Dax. The moment he heard her say his name, his hands steadied to a slight quiver, and he told her the whole story.

"Wow, that's intense!" she said, falling onto her bed. School had been out for almost three hours, and she had just finished her English essay on the effects of technology in modern society.

"It was," Zax said, sounding as if he had already lost.

"Is everything ok?"

"Yeah, it's ok. I'm just worried that I won't be strong enough to defeat Dax. I used everything I had. Any wound I gave him immediately healed as if nothing had happened. I literally hit him with a bolt of lightning, and he treated it like a mosquito."

"I'm so sorry," she said, hearing the discouragement in his voice. Hoping to make him feel better, she decided to take a stab at lightening his concern by poking fun at herself.

"Hey, if you can't take him down, I will. He better not underestimate me if he doesn't want to get taken down in one hit."

Zax smiled. "True. No one should underestimate you. I mean, you scare me sometimes when you get really angry."

"Hey!" she said, softly laughing, and knew it had worked, even if for only a moment.

When she stopped laughing, there was a brief silence on the line before he spoke again. Softly and sincerely, he said, "Thank you, Jaiden. I seriously needed that. You always know how to make everything better." With her on his side, he knew he could do anything. His heart was full. Any worry he had about Dax had been thrown out the window.

"Anytime," she whispered.

Just then, Walter busted into the hallway. "We think we know how to make you stronger," he shouted excitedly, waving some papers above his head.

"Hey Jaiden, I need to go. They think they found something."

"Ok, go take him down. I know you can do it!"

"I promise. I'll defeat him."

Before Zax left the hallway to follow Walter, he closed his eyes. Once again, he copied himself with the energy and sent it to Jaiden the same way he had when he'd brought her home from school without being there. As soon as he could see her in her room through the eyes of the duplicate energy, he hugged her. She hugged back. She loved the fact that she could physically feel him despite being somewhere else.

He smiled and returned the energy puppet back into the earth and back to him.

"Since when could you do that?" Walter asked as he saw a translucent copy of Zax's form come from out of nowhere and sink into the ground.

"We don't have time for questions," Zax said, grinning.

"Maybe not now, but definitely later," Walter said, turning to go back inside the room he'd come from. Zax followed close behind. It was the same room where he had been introduced to Dr. Citlali.

Dr. Citlali was standing near a table stacked high with manilla folders when they entered the room. Anxiously, Zax asked, "What is it? You think you found something?"

"It is a theory," Dr. Citlali said, "but...I have been looking into all the passages that mention 'spark' from multiple cultures. They all mention the same thing, yet in different ways. Basically, long version short, more power requires more strength."

Dr. Citlali picked up a loose paper off the table and began reading it aloud. "If you increase your physical strength, you may be able to increase how much energy you use relative to how strong the energy is. The energy you possess and use at this level of physical strength is, in that moment, at its maximum. But if you increase that physical strength, you can also increase your energy strength, which makes sense if you really think about it. Every living creature gives off some electrical charge. It is too weak, of course, to be used by regular humans.

"When some people who aren't healthy die, we say they died from natural causes, like a heart attack. But it can be because they got upset or scared. The truth is, if Dax's story is true, then every living thing has at least a little bit of the energy inside the core of the earth."

Dr. Citlali looked directly at Zax. "And as we know, your energy is derived from how strong your emotions are. These heart attacks are the people who are too weak to use the energy. They get whiplashed from unintentionally trying to use the small amount of energy inside them."

"So, if what you say is true, Dr. Citlali…Dax's body is made up of his energy, and he doesn't have any muscles to tear and rebuild. But Zax does," Walter said, turning to Zax.

"Meaning that I can become stronger than Dax, both physically and energy-wise."

"Exactly!" Walter said.

"But to become stronger than Dax, we don't have time to wait for my muscles to repair every time I work out."

Dr. Citlali, realizing he was no longer part of this exchange, walked to the chalkboard and began analyzing calculations.

"Well, we finally realized something that happens when you use the energy recharge room," Walter said. "I don't know why it took so long, but every time you recharge, your wounds and stamina are healed and replenished. And, technically, torn muscles from exercising are a type of wound."

Zax thought for a moment. "So basically, I'll go work out until I'm completely exhausted and can't keep going, then I'll go to the recharge room and recharge. And I should be as good as new? I'll already be a little stronger from the workout, but I can go straight back to working out since I won't have to worry about the muscles taking days to repair themselves. Is that what you're saying?"

"You took the words right out of my mouth," Walter said. "Only one problem. You'll need a trainer, and we don't have one right now. Everyone here, including myself, is too busy to take it on."

"What about Jack?" Zax asked without hesitation. "He played football, so he must know a little about physical training. And maybe I can get Jaiden to be my workout buddy?"

"Sounds reasonable. Think you can get in touch with him?" Walter asked. "If Jack and Jaiden want to be a part of your training, I'll talk with the director and get them clearance."

"Then we have a plan?"

"We do. Why don't you go talk to Jack and see what he says. But come back as soon as possible. You need to get to work immediately, and Dr. Citlali does too. He thinks there's another thing missing."

Walter looked over at Dr. Citlali's scribbles on the chalkboard. "While you train, he'll continue his research."

39

Zax left The Office and headed to the small one-story brick house at 97 Marshall Street, where Jack lived. It was the third house on the left and the only house on the street with a pergola supported by exposed beams covering the concrete porch. He could see the white house number attached to the reddish brown, windowless front door from the driveway.

He stepped onto the narrow porch and knocked on the door, hoping Jack would answer. He wasn't sure if this was the correct address and didn't really have time to make a mistake—like misspelling the street name in the GPS.

But it wasn't Jack who opened the door. A little girl with blonde pigtails and green eyes peered through a small, open crack in the door.

"Hey there, is Jack home?" Zax asked as he crouched down to her eye level.

"Stranger danger!!!" the little girl screamed, slamming the door in his face.

Zax fell and landed on his back. Stunned, he rolled over onto his stomach and got on all fours, facing away from the door. Just as he was about to stand, the door swung wide open and Jack—with a football in his hand—was ready for attack.

Seeing nothing other than what appeared to be an unknown person on their hands and knees, Jack threw the football at the back of Zax's head. Zax fell back down, face first this time, onto the porch.

"Hey Jack, it's me," Zax said as he turned over and rubbed the back of his head. "Bet the team wishes you were still playing."

"Oh my gosh, I didn't know it was you," Jack said and extended his hand to help him up. "When my little sister screamed, I shot up thinking you were an intruder or a salesman."

"Why would you throw a football at a salesman?" Zax asked, laughing.

"First impressions are everything."

I guess that's one way to keep salesmen from coming back twice, Zax thought.

"Jack, watch out! He's a stranger," the little girl yelled, hiding behind the door. "Throw the ball at him again!"

"Sally, this isn't a stranger. This is Zax. He's a friend from school. Come here."

Sally slowly came from behind the door to get a better look at Zax. "I'm sorry. I didn't know you were friends with my brother. I'm not supposed to open the door, but I did."

"It's ok, don't worry about it," Zax said.

She stared at him for a few seconds, then ran past him into the yard to grab the football that had bounced off his head. With the ball in her hand, she ran back inside and closed the door.

"So, what are you doing here?" Jack asked. "More importantly, are you ok? Jaiden told me something happened with you and Dax, but she didn't give me any details."

"I'm fine, but I may have a headache later," he joked, still rubbing the back of his head. The truth was, there was no doubt he was going to have a headache. Probably sooner than later. Jack had not lost his touch with a football. "As for Dax, that's why I'm here. I wanted to tell you what happened and ask you for a favor. Is it ok if we walk while we're talking?"

"Yeah, sure. Just a sec." Jack poked his head inside. "Hey Sally, I'll be back in a few minutes. Why don't you grab the iPad and play a game or watch something? And lock the door. Don't open it unless you see me. No one else."

"Ok," she said.

He watched as Sally picked up the iPad off the ottoman and waited until he heard the lock click before he went to meet Zax at the end of his driveway.

Walking down the fully shaded, oak-lined street, Zax told him everything that had happened in Antarctica and what Dr. Citlali had found so far.

"Wow! Ok. So maybe I shouldn't have bullied you. I mean, you being the reason why any of us are here and all," Jack said with an awkward laugh.

"All that is in the past. Forgiven and forgotten. Technically speaking, it wasn't me who made the world. It was the energy. It just kind of, I guess, chose me to use its power. I don't really know to be honest."

Jack didn't know what to say. He understood football, not energy or Dax or anything that Zax had just told him. He wanted to move on to something he might be able to grasp. "So, about this favor…"

"I could use your help with working out. I need a trainer and thought that you would know a thing or two about working out since you played football. The Office doesn't have anyone available. I also thought about asking Jaiden if she wanted to join in and be my workout partner or something. What do you think?"

"Are you kidding? Of course, I'll help you! And that's a great idea to ask Jaiden. It's easier to work out— and a lot more fun—when you have someone sharing the experience with you."

"Thanks, Jack. I knew I could count on you. By the way, you have a sister? I didn't know you had one. How old is she?"

"Yeah. Sally can be a handful sometimes, as you can tell. I have to look after her since our parents practically work all day and night. She's ten."

"Man, I wish I could help. Maybe sometimes I can come over to help you look after her. That is, as long as she doesn't slam the door in my face, and I don't get hit with another football." Zax grinned.

"Ha-ha. No promises there, but you can come by anytime."

40

Once they got back to his house, Jack called his parents and made sure it was all right for Sally to stay home alone for a little while. He told them that he had already talked to their next-door neighbor, Mrs. Ashby, and she told him that if Sally needed anything at all, she could call or come over. He also told them he would make her some mac and cheese with broccoli before he left. After a few minutes, he'd convinced them that they shouldn't worry.

When Sally's dinner was made, he told her to call Mrs. Ashby if she needed anything and to lock the door behind him. He opened the front door to leave and told her not to open it for anyone other than him, Mrs. Ashby, or their mom and dad. She gave him a thumbs up.

While Jack had been lining everything up for Sally, Zax waited by his car and called Jaiden. He told her that Jack had agreed to be his trainer and hoped she would, and could, be his workout partner. She put him on hold while talking to her parents. Ten minutes later, she returned with good news. They thought it was a great idea. They were both fitness buffs and had been encouraging her to be more

active. Until now, she had shown no interest, so they were
thrilled.

Chapter 10
Breaking Limits

Dennis Eaves

Part 41

After hanging up with Jaiden, Zax called Walter and told him to go ahead and get the clearances for both Jack and Jaiden as soon as he could. Everything was falling into place.

"You think Jaiden's parents will let her go?" Jack asked as he opened the passenger's side door of the Malibu.

"We're headed there now," Zax smiled and started the car. "They usually let her do something if she really wants to."

When they pulled into her driveway, Jaiden was sitting on the front porch steps with a purple duffle bag at her feet. She hopped into the backseat, and the three of them took off for The Office and their first workout session. It was crucial they get started immediately.

As they pulled into the office's parking lot, it occurred to Zax that this was the first time either of them had been there.

"Is this it?" Jaiden asked, surprised, staring at the blah, nondescript building. "This is not what I was expecting based on all the talk of the place!"

"Looks like it could use a major upgrade," Jack laughed.

"I thought the same thing the first time I saw it. It looks bland on the outside but wait until you see the inside…that's where all the cool stuff is," Zax said. "Come on, and I'll show you around."

They got out of the car, and Zax punched in his code to gain access to the building. "Walter was able to get security clearance for both of you from our director, Alvin. To be honest, I'm surprised that he approved it. He can be a stick in the mud sometimes. We'll go see him after I give you a quick tour of the building. He'll tell us where we can do the workouts. I'm sure it'll be somewhere other than the classified areas."

After wandering through the building for about twenty minutes, they made their way to the director's office. Once introductions were made, it was time to address why they were there.

"Oh, the gym isn't here. It's in a different location." Director Alvin leaned back in his office chair, propped his feet up on his desk, and crossed his arms. "It's still a part of The Office. It's just not in this building. It's down the road, within walking distance."

"You mean the tan building? The one with the fence?" Zax was puzzled. He had been coming to The Office for a long time and never once suspected it was part of their campus. "I was told that was a private gym."

"Sorry we misled you. Most of our agents don't even know it's ours. We use it for specialized training only. And only our special-ops agents have access. That is, until now. I've decided to grant you three access. But know this…" He put his feet down and leaned forward on his desk. With a stern warning, he said, "Speaking of this facility outside of my office will result in serious consequences. Do you understand?"

Zax looked at Jaiden and Jack, then back at Director Alvin. "Yes, sir," he said. "We understand."

The director stood up and walked to the front of his desk. "Jaiden. Jack. It was nice meeting you both. Just don't forget, what you see and do here, stays here. You don't want to find out what happens if it doesn't."

Jaiden and Jack nodded. They wondered what they had just stepped into.

42

The three of them left the director's office and headed out to see exactly what was so secretive that only a handful of agents had been privy to.

"He didn't seem like a stick in the mud to me," Jack said, kicking a pebble off the road. "Maybe a little scary and intense."

"Try working with him for a year when the most interaction you two have had is with a gun in the face," Zax replied.

"I can see your point." Jack pointed at the building to their left. "Is this where we're going?"

"It is."

Zax studied the tan building as they got closer, looking for anything that might have clued him in. He wondered if Ethan and Jenny knew about this place and why, after everything he'd done for them, Director Alvin had kept him in the dark.

By all appearances, the tan building was an exclusive, high-end gym that provided the utmost privacy for its clientele. A wrought iron security fence enclosed the perimeter, and two security guards manned the electronic gate, twenty-four seven. No one was getting in without proper credentials. The closer they got, the more Zax wondered how he had never found this suspicious.

"Welp," Zax said as they reached the security gate. "Let's go in and take a look."

Holding up their lanyards that displayed their name, date of birth, and scannable barcode, the security guards quickly verified that the director had, himself, given them clearance for entry. Once satisfied, the wrought iron gate opened, allowing Zax, Jaiden, and Jack passage. As the gate closed behind them, the door to the building automatically opened.

Jaiden could feel her heart pounding as they crept toward their destination. The front of the building was lined with one-way glass windows and a heavy metal door. No one could see in, but everyone could see out. Her heartbeat became deafening as the security door slammed behind them.

Noticing her anxiety, Zax took her hand. "Are you ok?"

"I think so." She held on tightly as they scoured the room.

At first glance, the one-story room looked like any other gym. It was filled with treadmills, bench presses, free weights, and a host of other exercise equipment. But when Zax saw the elevator in the back of the room, he realized that this place was a lot more than what it seemed; it told him all he needed to know. This place was like his house. It had multiple levels leading underground. In addition, there was only one occupant other than them in the room. And she stood in front of the elevator.

"You must be Zax," the five-foot-four agent said. Her brown hair was pulled into a bun on top of her head, adding at least two inches to her height. She wore darkly tinted sunglasses that kept her eyes hidden and a black suit with a white collared button-up shirt and tie. Basic agent dress code, even in the middle of spring.

"My name is Agent Tonya. I'm here to bring you to the special training area. We're confident that this will get you physically strong in no time. We will be going to the lowest level, Level 6. Levels 1 through 3 have equipment that is inferior to what you have in your house. Levels 4 and 5 are equivalent to what you have with hologram training, etcetera. And then there's Level 6. In this area, you'll find top-of-the-line high-tech training equipment, a food bar that will only give you what you need—only when you need it—and a smaller recharge room. We have a recharge room here, so you don't have to go to the main office and back over and over. It was originally a prototype of a portable recharge room for you to use on the field if needed. It should work well enough to heal the wounds."

Zax, Jaiden, and Jack looked at each other with apprehension as Tonya turned to place her security key into a slot on the side of the elevator. When it arrived, she held the door open and motioned for everyone to get in, then pressed a non-labeled button on the front wall. A glass panel slid to the side, and another button emerged. This button showed the number six. Agent Tonya pressed that button, and the elevator slowly started to descend.

"So, do you have a workout list or something?" Zax whispered to Jack.

"No. I need to see the equipment and what kind of schedule this food bar works on. I also need to see how much you can handle before I can make a proper list," Jack whispered back. "And to be honest, I think you can handle a lot. You threw me across a room one time, and that was a year ago. You've only become stronger since then."

The elevator dinged, indicating they had arrived at Level 6. "Here we are," Agent Tonya announced without stepping off. "You'll need to hit the button labeled 'Level 1' when you're finished. This will take you directly back to the main level. Do not hit any other button. Got it?"

They nodded. "Now get to work," she said and shooed them into the room.

Once the elevator doors closed and Agent Tonya was gone, Zax and Jaiden breathed a sigh of relief; Jack, on the other hand, gasped in amazement at the sight of all the different, unique equipment in the room.

With widened eyes and an even wider smile, Jack said, "What?! This isn't possible. You're pulling my leg!"

"What do you mean?" Zax asked.

Jack was hardly able to contain his excitement. "There's equipment here that hasn't even been released to the public, but you have like three of each! With all this stuff, going non-stop and doing the recharge, I would say that you would be double your current strength in a week or two."

"We need a lot more than double since I don't know how long we have until Dax wants to fight."

"Well, if we push you past what you can handle and get you to the recharge immediately…and it heals all your wounds, including your torn muscles, and lets them rebuild to give you all your stamina back…then we can probably half the time to a few days in terms of doubling your strength. A week on the outside. But that's only if you and I have nothing else to do and do it around the clock."

"Around the clock? Meaning…" Zax thought Jack was being literal, but he wanted to make sure.

"Just that. We stay here until it's done," Jack replied. "We can sleep and eat, of course. But beyond that, we train."

"I have nothing to do. I'm all in for staying here, but what about your sister? She can't stay by herself for that long. Can your parents get a babysitter?" Zax asked. "Do you think they will let you stay here and miss school?"

Before Jack could respond, Jaiden chimed in. "What about Mark? He doesn't have a job, and believe it or not, he's really good with kids. He could stay with her after school. Would that work?"

"Uh, are you sure that's a good idea?" Zax asked, remembering how Sally slammed the door in his face and he got pounded with a football.

"Totally," Jaiden said. "I'll give him a call later. So Jack, do you think you can sell something to your parents? Think they'll agree to let you miss school? Maybe you could say you're going on a trip or something. I think I'm going to be straight up with my parents. If we can get Walter to set up the same arrangement with the school that Zax has, they'll agree. They're pretty cool that way, especially if it's something I really want to do and has to do with working out."

"I know what I'm going to tell them." Jack looked around the room. "One question…where are we going to sleep? Surely not in here. On second thought, maybe we should just go back home at night?"

"No, you were right. We need all the time here we can get. Driving back and forth from each of our houses would eat way too much of our training time. Besides, why can't we sleep in here? We can use sleeping bags." Zax caught a strange look from Jaiden and Jack. "What? Have you never gone camping before?"

"Uh, no," Jack said.

"At my old school, we went on a camping trip, but we stayed in a cabin with beds and air conditioning," Jaiden said.

"It's not that bad. I used to do it all the time back at my old house." Zax smiled. "At least we have AC, right?"

Jack looked at the bench press and then the floor. "I think I'll just get a blanket and sleep on the bench."

"I'm guessing that would be worse or more uncomfortable than the floor, but do whatever you want," Zax shrugged.

"Yeah…well, I think I'll just sleep on the bench press," Jack laughed.

43

Jaiden had found her way to the water fountain and was on her way back when Zax turned around and saw, for a split second, the same face she'd had on the plane traveling to California for their field trip, the trip where he'd battled the brute. The "you better sleep with one eye open" look she'd given Mark was not something he'd forgotten. Over the last year, he'd learned to recognize it all too well.

He laughed, though confused. *Why would she have that look just because Jack wanted to sleep on the bench press?*

"I'm going to call Mark," she said, brushing past them. The two of them looked at each other and shrugged their shoulders. Zax knew that whatever was irritating her would pass. It always did.

While Jaiden was off calling Mark about watching Sally and calling her Mom, Jack called his parents and told them that Zax had asked him to go on a road trip with him to visit a distant relative. Seeing this relative was going to be difficult, he said, and Zax really needed his support. Technically, Jack wasn't lying. Dax was a relative; he just was not human.

Jack had an answer for every question his mom and Dad threw at him. Mark was going to watch Sally after school at no charge; Mrs. Ashby agreed to be a backup; he'd made arrangements with the school to get his assignments and turn them in with no penalty. Though he had not confirmed any of these things, he hoped he could, without any glitches. After much hesitation, they told him they admired his devotion to his friend and were proud of how he managed his responsibilities. They agreed to let him go. *I hope we can do everything I just told them, or else they are going to be pissed!* he thought as he hung up the phone.

Things were falling into place when Jaiden and Jack met back up with Zax. Mark had agreed to watch Sally, and her parents said yes, as she had predicted. The final piece of pulling this off was getting Walter to call the school, which he did willingly. The school agreed to the same terms they had agreed upon for Zax. Everything would be fine if Jack and Jaiden turned their work in before the end of the six weeks.

Jack borrowed Zax's car to grab a few things from home and introduce Mark to Sally. Though Mark lived on the street behind Jack and had seen Sally around the neighborhood, they had never been properly introduced. Jack knew Sally would like Mark; everyone did.

Zax and Jaiden stayed behind to power up some of the equipment and check things out. With Jack gone, Zax felt like he could finally ask her about the look she'd thrown

Jack when they had talked about where to sleep. It had been messing with his head since he had seen it.

"Hey Jaiden, why did you make your 'you better sleep with one eye open' face at Jack?"

"What?" she said and looked over his shoulder at the dumbbell rack. "I have no clue what you're talking about."

"You're not good at lying. Just tell me."

"Fine. I guess you couldn't tell, but Jack was about to change his mind and decide to sleep on the floor instead of the bench press. I wanted to sleep next to you, just you and me, no one else. Kind of like our own world or something." She looked down at the floor. "I know it sounds—"

"You're too cute," he whispered and lifted her head. "But Jack could just sleep on the other side of the room or something."

"Yeah, I guess so," she whispered back. "I love you so much."

He smiled at the thought of them sleeping side by side. "And I love you too." He wrapped his arms around her and kissed her, holding her close.

44

"So, you ready to get started?" Jack asked as he walked back into the exercise room.

"As soon as possible," Zax answered. "How did things go with Mark?"

"It's all good. I think they'll do fine. Mark and Sally immediately hit it off. They just met, and they're like the best of friends." Without batting an eye, he added, "Let's do it."

Jack led Zax and Jaiden across the room to the far-left corner, opposite the elevator, to the DC Profile 1000 Butterfly Machine, a state-of-the-art weight machine explicitly designed to strengthen the pectoral muscles. Though he was familiar with this type of equipment, as he studied it, he noticed the design had an added feature he'd never seen. Not only could weight be added or lessened by the cabled blocks behind the seat, the cable itself, had clamps that could increase or decrease resistance to the weights adding more difficulty. In addition, the arms on the machine could rotate such that the user's arms could be pulled together from a horizontal position or diagonally rotated to any angle other than a full ninety.

"This is so cool!" Jack walked around the equipment, carefully studying and admiring every part. "And look at those padded arm supports!" he said, feeling the machine.

In all the time that Zax had known Jack, he'd never seen him this excited about anything.

"Ok, sit down," Jack said. "Let's get to work."

"Let's go."

Zax sat down on the upright bench and slid his arms into the adjustable three-sided arm sleeves. They extended from the wrist to the elbow and left the portion of the user's arm that faced inward, exposed. He was ready to begin.

Jack gave him some pointers on form, what to expect, and the specific muscles that would be worked. Jaiden stood on the other side of the machine, listening intently. Once correctly positioned, Jack went behind the machine and set Zax's lifting weight at five hundred pounds with an added twenty percent resistance on the clamps. Since he was already physically strong because of the energy, he lifted with ease. After three sets of seventy-five reps, Jaiden took his place.

She giggled nervously as she sat down in the seat. She had never used any exercise equipment before. Jack restated the correct form and then adjusted the weight level to ninety-five pounds with no resistance. Surprisingly, she did ten reps per set without any trouble.

"Good job, Jaiden," Zax congratulated and held his hand up for a high-five.

"Yeah," Jack added. "Pretty impressive for someone as small as you."

Jaiden smiled and high-fived Zax's hand as she got off the butterfly press, and they walked over to the next upper body challenge, the bench press.

"I can't believe this equipment!" Jack said. "I can't wait to try this stuff out myself!"

"Remember, we need to stay on track," Zax said, trying to snap Jack out of his fantasyland.

The DC Profile 2000 Bench Press looked like a traditional press in that it had a bench that could lie flat, incline, or decline, with a lifting bar that allowed Olympic weight plates to be added. But, like the butterfly press, the bar also had a cable attached to both ends, allowing for more—or less—resistance by the placement of a clamp.

Zax laid flat on the bench as Jack loaded the same amount as the other machine, five hundred pounds, onto the bar. However, here he set the additional resistance at only ten percent. Once the weights were in place, and with Jack spotting him, Zax reached up and grabbed the bar. He lifted it off the rack, then lowered it to his chest and lifted it back up. By the time he had finished and placed the bar back in its holding rack, he had lifted fifty reps on each of the bench press variations—the traditional bench press, the incline, and the decline.

When it came time for Jaiden, she lifted eighty pounds, seven times with zero resistance, but only lying flat. No inclines or declines. Jack and Zax agreed, once again, that it was pretty impressive what she could do.

From there, they ditched the equipment and walked to the front corner of the room, next to the elevator. Mats were rolled out on the floor, and weighted clothes hung from a hook on the wall. Zax took them from the hangers and put them over his training clothes. Jaiden declined. Zax, with added resistance, and Jaiden, without, continued their workout with sit-ups, crunches, mountain climbers, and other exercises that targeted their torso, chest, back, and core. Zax did eighty sit-ups, seventy-six crunches, and ninety mountain climbers, while Jaiden completed fifty sit-ups, forty-three crunches, and fifty-eight mountain climbers.

With the upper body rotation complete, they moved to the lower body. The leg press and the inner/outer thigh machines were much like the bench press and butterfly machine in that they had adjustable weights and resistance clamps. Zax did seventy-four reps at three hundred fifty-one pounds with twenty percent resistance on the thigh machine and sixty reps at four hundred pounds with twenty percent resistance on the leg press, all without using any energy. Jaiden did eleven reps at fifty-nine pounds on the thigh machine and ten reps on the leg press at eighty pounds.

After squats, lunges, and step-ups, they ended the first set on the treadmills. Running side-by-side for thirty minutes—Zax at fifteen miles per hour and Jaiden at six—it was time to move back to position one, the butterfly press.

After they completed the second full round, Jaiden had to take a break. Not quit, just take a small break to catch her breath. She wanted to quit, but she knew that for Zax's sake, she couldn't. He needed her support; he needed her to be his partner. Since bailing wasn't an option for him, she couldn't either. She was going to have to settle for lightening the weights and slowing her pace. First, though, she had to take a breather.

With no objection from Zax or Jack, they walked to the open mat area in front of the free-weight rack, laid down, and stared at the ceiling. For half an hour, Jack talked endlessly about the gym and its equipment. Zax and Jaiden remained mostly quiet.

"Alright, you two," Jack said and stood up. Standing between them as they continued to lie unmoved, he hovered over them and looked down at their faces. He nudged Zax's side with his foot. "We've got to keep at it. You ready?"

Zax and Jaiden shifted their eyes to his smiling face, then rolled over and got up. "You're enjoying this way too much," Jaiden said.

"I am, indeed!" Jack grinned, staring at them.

45

Rested and rehydrated, they pushed through sets three and four seemingly unscathed. But as Zax stepped off the treadmill after the fourth set, he suddenly felt like he was going to pass out and throw up at the same time, as if he was about to kick the bucket any second. Jack noticed his instability and exhaustion—he'd seen the same body movement many times on the football field—and rushed over, catching Zax before he collapsed onto the floor.

He ran Zax into the recharge room hoping that Dr. Citlali's prediction would prove to be correct. That he would regain his stamina, and his torn muscles would be repaired while making him stronger at the same time. He also hoped Walter was correct and that Zax's wounds would recover too. But since this recharge room had never been tested, they weren't a hundred percent confident of either.

Jake and Jaiden stood outside the recharge room and waited, nervous and worried. Neither spoke as they paced back and forth in front of the room.

Less than ten minutes later, Zax reemerged practically as good as new. The recharge room had worked.

Walter and Dr. Citlali had been right. His stamina was back, and his muscles were repaired and stronger than before.

Jaiden ran up to him and grabbed his hands. "Are you ok?"

"Yeah. I think so."

"You gave us quite a scare back there, you know," Jack said, trying to pretend like he hadn't been worried.

"Sorry about that. I know it's kind of scary the first time you experience it, but the good news is that I'm ready for more. The question is, are you ready?"

"Oh, yeah. I'm ready," Jack said and playfully punched Zax's shoulder. "Come on, Jaiden, let's see what he's got."

Zax and Jaiden did the entire workout, again and again, going through every exercise from the butterfly press to the treadmill. After each set, Zax went into the recharge room while Jaiden rested. Upon completion of the fourth set, Jaiden had to stop; she was exhausted. Zax continued until he had completed his seventh set, and then, collectively, they decided to call it a day. By the time they were done, Zax could do all the exercises with at least a hundred additional pounds, five percent more resistance, and five sets of eight or more reps. At that point, he felt like he would collapse onto the ground.

"I can't believe it worked that well!" Zax exclaimed and reached for a towel as he stepped out of the recharge.

"Me either. This is incredible! But then you have to remember you already have some really incredible powers, such as creating weapons from pure energy and, oh yeah, the ability to fly! Building muscles is the most normal thing you have done—if you exclude the assistance you get by use of the recharge," Jack said, amused.

"He has a point," Jaiden said.

"Yeah, I guess so. That was a pretty stupid thing to say, wasn't it?" Zax said and turned to Jaiden. "How are you feeling?"

"Oh, I'm fine. I couldn't keep up with you, though. Not even close."

"Well, as Jack said, I do have a crazy power."

"Yeah, but you didn't use it when you threw me across the room," Jack said. "Which still confuses me. Because even without the energy, you're still very physically strong. How come?"

"That's not completely true. I had to use a little of the power so the recharge room would actually recharge me. I've never used it to increase my strength or anything like that, only to constantly pump out a hair-thin stream of energy. When I threw you a year ago, I didn't have control over the energy; I didn't even know I had it. I guess my throwing you was a fight-or-flight reaction. It's just an addition that comes with the energy, I guess." The three of them pondered what he'd said for a few seconds. "Hey, I'm going to go out for a bit. Need anything?"

"We still have some of the pizza Walter sent over from earlier, so we're good," Jack said.

"Be safe," Jaiden said, hugging him.

"See ya," Jack said.

When the door closed behind Zax, Jack put his hands on his hips and looked around the room. "I can't believe I can only stay here two weeks. Hopefully, it'll last that long."

Jaiden rolled her eyes, then went to grab a slice of pizza and call her mom.

46

Feeling much stronger, Zax left the gym and drove back to his house. He still hadn't seen Ethan and Jenny since his return from the Arctic. But he had to be discrete since Jack's parents thought they were on a trip.

"Ethan? Jenny?" he yelled, entering through the back door to a dark house. "Are you home?"

When neither answered, and he could not find a hint of them anywhere around, he walked into the kitchen and mumbled, "Guess not." He assumed they were on a mission or something, and The Office had failed to tell him. Though he was disappointed and thought it would have been nice to see them, they weren't the reason he was there.

He grabbed an apple off the kitchen counter and took the elevator down to the giant room on the bottom floor, the third-level basement, where he could fight the three beasts as many times as he wanted. When he reached the control panel, he selected to battle eight of every beast simultaneously, which was more than he had ever tried.

The door on the other side of the room opened, and the beasts raced towards him. As they did, Zax took a bite out of the apple and tossed it high into the air. He quickly began to charge up the energy around his arm so much that little bits of electricity sparked off his arm. He thrust his arm out, and a massive wave of energy rushed toward the beasts. Without him going into the aura state, every beast in the room was wiped out instantly. And it all happened before he caught the apple as it fell back down. Nothing was left in the room but piles of purple ooze, himself, and a half-eaten apple.

"So, this exercise thing does work," Zax said as he looked at his hand before taking another bite of the apple. "Even so, this is nowhere near enough to stop Dax. Until I can do what I just did but take on eighty thousand of each beast, I don't think I'll be on his level. Let alone stronger than him."

The clock was ticking. Zax knew he had to continue getting stronger if he were to protect not only the people he cared about, but the entire world.

"Impressive. We know you can do it," a familiar voice said. He turned around. It was Ethan. And with him were Jenny, Walter, Jaiden, and Jack. Director Alvin trailed behind.

"I noticed the look on your face as you left the gym, the one you get when you're determined," Jaiden said. "So, I called everyone, and we followed you back here."

"We know you won't stop until you win," Jenny said. "You've always had a knack for getting up stronger after getting knocked down."

"You're too stubborn to lose to an evil being like Dax," Walter said. "You've shown me that no matter who you're up against, you don't let up or stand down."

"If you could deal with my bullying for as long as you did, then there's no way you can't deal with this Dax thing," Jack said.

"You've always dodged, deflected, and taken every hit I put in your direction, head-on. If anyone can defeat someone as powerful as Dax, it's you," Director Alvin said. "You were brave enough to stand up for people you didn't even know, like the agent who almost got shot by a stray bullet last year and the people who were attacked in the town. You've got what it takes."

"You're always stronger when you fight for other people, like against Professor Brian. That's how I know you will take down Dax, no sweat," Jaiden said.

Zax stood with an expression of shock and amazement on his face. He took a deep breath, then closed his eyes and lowered his head. "I will take down Dax no matter the cost. I will work hard to become stronger than ever before. Every day I will exercise and do research with Dr. Citlali to find any weak points that Dax may have."

He lifted his head and looked into the eyes of everyone in front of him. "And I will make sure he never hurts anyone else ever again."

Chapter 11

The Encounter

Dennis Eaves

Part 47

It had been a little over a week since Zax and Jaiden had started their daily, nonstop exercise regimen, and despite the intensity of the workouts, Zax had managed to power through. On the other hand, Jaiden had to stop after a couple of days due to muscle fatigue and soreness. Zax had the advantage of the recharge room, while Jaiden's body had to repair its muscles on its own. The only time he had ever felt sore were the moments between stepping off the treadmill and entering the recharge room on day one after completing set four. The day he felt he could keel over at any second.

Zax's strength had increased exponentially and gone through the roof since they'd first started. He could now lift eight hundred pounds with fifty percent resistance on the butterfly press, seven hundred forty-six pounds with thirty percent resistance on the bench press, do a hundred ten sit-ups, ninety-four crunches, and a hundred twenty-three mountain climbers, all with the weighted clothes. He could now run twenty-eight miles per hour on the treadmill, lift seven hundred fifteen pounds on the leg press with fifty percent resistance, and nine hundred forty-eight pounds with sixty percent resistance on the thigh machine.

In addition to working out, Zax had begun working more closely with Dr. Citlali and his research team to develop new, plausible theories on how to defeat Dax. Since none of their initial theories proved to have any solid evidence and seeing that the religions which mentioned anything to do with Dax had been altered so much over time, they had to broaden their scope. Their early morning collaborations before Zax's workout—complete with lattes—had become a necessity.

They had to take a step back. They decided to try matching the information that Dax had relayed to Zax back in Antarctica with the religions that indirectly mention Dax. But all they found was that Dax had always been seen as some kind of destroyer or ultimate evil and that Zax and Dax had always been at each other's throats. No matter what avenue they pursued, they still had little to no information on how to defeat Dax or even a weakness to exploit.

48

A few days later, as Zax, Jaiden, and Jack had just left their morning meeting with Dr. Citlali and were walking toward the gym, a sudden, strange, foreboding sensation came over Zax. It was so intense that it took his breath and made him stop moving; it was a feeling of overwhelming malaise and murderous intent.

Jack and Jaiden took a few more steps before they realized he wasn't beside them anymore. They turned around and saw him standing still. But they saw no fear in his face. His unsmiling face was serious, and he looked ready for whatever was about to be thrown at him.

"Hey, what's up?" Jaiden asked.

"Something is coming, and it's not good."

"Is it Dax?!" Jack asked, panicked. "Is it finally time?"

"Let's hope not. I'm still not ready," Zax said, strangely calm. He looked in the direction of this sinister feeling. "I might have more of a chance since our encounter in Antarctica, but it's still not enough to keep up with him, let alone beat him."

Before they knew what was happening, there was a loud rumble, and Dax was right in front of them. Following him was a colossal gust of wind which caused random trees along the path to be ripped from the ground by their roots. He wanted Zax to know how fast he really was. When he flew at top-notch speeds, he was faster than the speed of sound, creating a sonic boom and tornado-like wave of air disturbance.

Dax's body had changed. He now looked almost human, and the features of his face were clear and devilish. His body was covered in the same purple energy as it was the first time he'd met Zax, but with more detail of "muscles"—fake in appearance—and his feet were oddly deformed. Immediately the air around him was filled with a terrible, vile odor and smelled of death. There was one thing that was certain. Everything about him was pure evil.

Jack and Jaiden froze, but Zax was trigger-happy. He encased his fist with a layer of energy and launched a punch at Dax's face. With the added energy, the impact was vastly more powerful than a regular punch.

Dax went flying and crashed into the ground a couple of yards behind where he was initially standing. "You have become stronger," Dax said as he stood and dusted himself off calmly, trying to show that the punch didn't hurt him.

"Yeah, so what?" Zax responded. "Is our battle starting now?"

"No. You still aren't ready," Dax answered. He returned to the same place he'd been before Zax punched him. "I realized I hadn't given you a time or place for our final momentous battle."

"Well, spit it out. Seeing your face and smelling your disgusting stench annoys me," Zax scowled. He made a fist like the one he had made when fighting the beasts back in the basement, and it started to emit electricity. "I might get trigger-happy again."

"Oh, so rude," Dax chuckled, staring Zax in the face. "The battle will be four weeks from today and will take place in the thermosphere above Mount Everest. It's the closest we can get to our previous battleground without you suffocating from a lack of oxygen. Well, as long as you go into your aura mode or whatever it is that you call it."

"How do you even know what or where Mount Everest is?"

"Because I was the one who watched it first form all those years ago in the prison you put me in. But payback is coming," Dax said in a confident tone as if he already knew he would win the fight. He started to levitate slowly. "Well, that's all I came to say. I'll be on my way now."

"Hold on." Zax transformed into the aura mode and rose to Dax's level. "Have you hurt anyone, or will you hurt anyone before our fight?"

"No. I decided I should let your little creations watch me destroy you before I destroy them. Or maybe I will have fun with them and rule over them or torture them. Who knows? I guess it will depend on my mood once I have defeated you," Dax answered with an ominous grin.

"One more question. Why are you letting me get stronger?"

"Well, I want an actual challenge. It doesn't really matter if you are stronger than me. Because unless you discover a way to defeat me permanently, then I will kill you," Dax said, still grinning. "See you on Mount Everest in four weeks on that peak. Where our fate, written in stone, shall be fulfilled. And where I shall dig your grave."

With that, Dax flew off with the same speed and force he had as he arrived. They watched him fly away, and when he was entirely out of sight, Jaiden and Jack rushed over to Zax's side as he descended back to the ground.

"What was that about?" Jack asked anxiously.

"Does he want to fight now?" Jaiden asked, just as anxious.

"No. He wanted to tell me when and where he wants to fight," Zax said. "He wants to fight in four weeks in the thermosphere of the Earth above Mount Everest."

"Why there?" Jack asked.

"Yeah, that's very specific," Jaiden said.

"According to him, it's the closest place to where our last battle was. But I have another theory that I need to talk to Dr. Citlali about," Zax said. "For now, let's just get to our workout. I need to channel this anger."

"I'll have to tell my parents that something came up, and the trip is going to be longer than expected," Jack said.

"I'll have to tell mine, too," Jaiden said.

"You two can go back home if you want or if you need to."

"And leave you with all the fun?" Jack said. "No way."

"You just want to be around the workout equipment, don't you?" Jaiden said, looking at Jack.

"Well, that too," Jack smiled.

"Thank you, guys. I really appreciate it." Jack gave Zax a thumbs-up, and Jaiden gave him a hug.

49

After another five hours of the same workout, Zax told Jaiden and Jack that he needed to go talk to Dr. Citlali and Walter about the encounter they'd had on the way to the gym; they needed to know everything.

Jaiden ran up behind him just as he reached out to press the call button on the elevator. "Can I come with you?"

"Of course. Does Jack want to come too, or did you scare him like you did last week with your look?"

"Why do you ask?"

"Because I see him cowering in that corner." Zax laughed and pointed to a punching bag that Jack was peeping around. Jaiden turned around and started laughing as well. "Come on. Let's go."

Just before they stepped onto the elevator, Zax yelled across the room, "Don't worry, Jack, I'll take the scary girl away."

"Thank you," Jack said with a sigh of relief and came out from hiding.

50

The sun was starting to set, and a light breeze blew as they stepped out of the tan building and walked toward The Office.

"We haven't had a moment alone like this since Dax first showed up," Zax said, taking her hand.

"I know."

"What's wrong? You sound so sad."

"Well, like you said, we haven't had a moment alone since Dax showed up, and in four weeks, you will battle him. He shrugged off your strongest attack. What if this is the last time we're alone together?"

"I understand your worry but don't go killing me off just yet. I've become a lot stronger since then," Zax said, trying to comfort her. "I mean, that punch this morning was my weakest. I would have to do a normal punch without the energy to make it any weaker. But it did, actually, send him flying. I know he was holding back, but that punch proves my training is working."

"Didn't he say that you can't beat him unless you can take him out permanently?"

"Yes. And I know how to do it," Zax said. "That's what we're going to talk to Dr. Citlali about."

"You mentioned you had another theory," she said and stopped walking. "But what if it's wrong, Zax?"

He turned to face her and smiled. "Then we find another way until it's not just a theory, but a fact."

Jaiden lowered her head and stared down at her feet. He put his hand on her chin and gently lifted her head. "Hey, how about I make a promise," he said softly.

"What do you mean?"

"What if I make a promise to come back? Have I ever broken one of our promises?"

"No, but that doesn't mean you will come back."

"I'm not done. Not with life and certainly not with you. By the time the fight comes, it will almost be graduation. After we both graduate, how about we finally make our lives together? We can get a house and possibly even get married," he said with a nervous laugh. "Actually, that was a dumb thing to say." *I can't believe I mentioned marriage out loud!* He spun around and started walking again, trying to escape what he had just said.

"No, it wasn't. If you can make me that promise, it will make me feel a thousand times better," she said, smiling and crying at the same time.

Zax stopped walking and went back to where she was standing. He pulled her in and kissed her longer than ever before. Then, brushing the tears from her cheek, he smiled and said, "Ok. I promise that I will come back and make a life with you."

51

When they got to The Office building, they went straight to Dr. Citlali's office. Hearing the knock on the door casing of the open door, Walter and Dr. Citlali looked up. Walter was sitting at Dr. Citlali's desk shuffling through reports, and Dr. Citlali stood beside him, reviewing his files. Walter was there trying to come up with his own theories as to how they were going to defeat Dax.

"What are you doing here?" Walter looked at the clock on the wall, surprised to see them this late; they had already had their daily meeting. From the expression on Zax's face, he wasn't sure he wanted to know. "Everything alright?"

Zax glanced over at Jaiden and then told Walter and Dr. Citlali about his encounter with Dax earlier in the day.

"Why didn't you come straight back?!" Walter asked.

"After it happened, I was too riled up to think logically, so I put all that energy and anger into the workout," Zax said. "But I now have a theory about Dax's weakness and how to stop him for good."

"What is it?" Dr. Citlali asked calmly.

"I think the only way to defeat Dax is to try and merge him with the energy in the core of the Earth," Zax said. "He wants to fight in the highest level of the atmosphere where I can still breathe while still having the largest amount of rock between us and the core— Mount Everest. It's the tallest place in the world and has the most rock. It's as if he's terrified of it or something."

"What if Dax knew you would think of that?" Walter asked. "And if you try to merge him with the core, he could take control of you or blow up the Earth."

"No," Zax answered. "If you remember, at the beginning of all of this, when the energy in the center of the Earth took control of me, it told us that Dax was smart when it came to survival, but he was not battle-wise. Dax wouldn't choose someplace so specific unless it had to do with him surviving the battle. He thinks that by putting as much rock between our fight and the core as he can, he will survive this fight. The only way he won't survive is if he's closer to the core, with less rock between us. Even though he is being stupid and cocky and making every mistake."

"What do you mean?" Jaiden asked.

"Well, he says that he witnessed Mount Everest forming. But if he really saw it form, he would not have chosen it as our place of battle. The truth about Mount Everest is that it's a volcano. The public isn't aware of this; they think it's a mountain and have classified it as such because it's dormant and has a zero percent chance of ever erupting again. But it's hollow down the center like any other volcano with a vent that leads into magma."

"Yes, but again, what if he takes control? Maybe that wasn't his intention, but maybe he still can," Walter said.

"If I can weaken him enough, the energy could overwhelm him. And instead of him taking over me, I could take over him."

"You said he made multiple mistakes. What are the other ones?" Jaiden asked.

"Making the battlefield so obvious to his weakness was one of his mistakes. But the biggest mistake he made was underestimating me. He thinks he is extremely powerful—and he is—but after four more weeks of training, I'm sure that I'll be stronger than him. Or at least as strong. He thinks all of this is a game and that he's stronger because he has all his energy at his disposal. I mean, he thought that even before the fight we supposedly had, which led to the Earth being made in the first place. Billions of years ago."

"This is still all just a theory. Do you have any proof?" Dr. Citlali asked.

"Yes, actually, I do. You know yin and yang, right? That's the closes thing that would describe Dax and me. Dark and light always being in balance. But if there is too much of one, it will take over the other. If I can weaken

Dax enough and force him into the core of the Earth, then light should be able to take over the dark."

"But according to yin and yang, that's not a good thing either. There always has to be dark as well, or there is no balance," Dr. Citlali said.

"Well, like you said when we first looked into this, the religions have been altered so much that maybe it isn't even true," Zax said. "Maybe to create balance, Dax has to merge with the core."

"That's a really big maybe," Walter said.

"Does anyone have a better idea?" Zax asked, starting to lose his patience. "There was another thing he said. He said he may not immediately kill all humans but rather toy with them first. I could tell he was being serious. Trust me, making him merge with the core is the only way to defeat him."

No one said a thing.

"I think Zax is right," Jaiden finally said. "After his explanation, it makes sense."

"I agree. Jaiden has a point," Dr. Citlali said, looking in her direction.

"Ok. So, I guess we have a plan then," Walter sighed.

Zax looked around at each of them. "I've made this promise before, and I'll make it again. I *will* take down Dax, no matter what."

Though they all feared for the uncertain future that lay ahead, they agreed that there was no choice but to send Zax into battle and trust him and his plan.

Dr. Citlali excused himself to take a call, and Jaiden left to grab a soda. When only Zax and Walter remained in the room, Zax walked over and closed the door.

"Hey Walter, I need to ask you a favor," Zax said.

Chapter 12
The Showdown

Dennis Eaves

Part 52

It had been a little less than four weeks since Dax had told Zax about the time and place for their battle. Two days remained until their face-off above Mount Everest.

Zax had exercised every day, five hours a day for five weeks, non-stop. After all his training, he now could lift over five thousand pounds on the butterfly press with one hundred percent resistance, bench four thousand eight hundred fifty-five pounds with the same resistance, do a thousand fifty sit-ups, a thousand twenty crunches, and a thousand eighty mountain climbers—all with the weighted clothes. He could run eighty-five miles per hour, lift four thousand seven hundred sixty-eight pounds on the thigh machine with total resistance, and five thousand one hundred and eighty pounds with total resistance on the leg press.

"So, this is it. The last time you get to do more strength training before battling Dax," Jack said to Zax. "Hope I haven't failed you."

"You haven't. I could've never done this without you," Zax said. "But yup, tomorrow is the day that determines what happens with the world, and only we, and The Office, will know that it is happening. I'm confident I'll defeat him, but just to be sure, I want to test one more thing."

Back at home, Zax went down to the bottom floor of the basement. He wanted to test what he could do against the three different beasts with his current strength. Everyone was there—Ethan, Jenny, Jaiden, Jack, Mark, Walter, and Director Alvin—to witness his newfound strength.

"I've got the remote control, and we're going to start with fifty thousand of every beast," Ethan said from the observation room.

"No. Do a hundred thousand of every beast," Zax said.

"Are you crazy? That's too dangerous! I'm not—"

"Do it. You can stop them with the remote if it gets out of hand."

Ethan looked at the others in the room, and they nodded. Though he was totally against the idea, he pressed the buttons on the controller. "Ok, fine. One hundred thousand it is."

The door on the other side of the room opened, and a hundred thousand of each beast rushed out and charged toward Zax. As before, he just stood there, letting them get closer and closer, the same way he had when Jaiden came to watch him train. The same way he had when there were only five of each beast.

He began to charge up the energy in his arm like he had with Dax. But this time, when the electricity flew off his arm, the lights in the basement and observation room began to flicker, and the panel that controlled the beasts, sparked and short-circuited. The remote in Ethan's hand could no longer control them.

Zax waited until the wild, uncontrollable beasts were only a few feet away from him before he lifted his arm and pushed out a giant, extremely powerful wave of the energy. Within seconds all the lights went out in the room; it was so powerful that everyone in the observation room thought the house was going to come crashing down. When the backup generator kicked on and the lights came back, they saw that every beast—all three hundred thousand— had been atomized. Not even a single trace of the purple substance was left behind.

Zax turned around and looked up into the observation room. Everyone, except Jaiden, stared blankly into the room that had, just moments ago, been filled to the brim with beasts who literally, within a blink of an eye, were gone. Her eyes were on Zax. She wasn't looking out into the room where the thousands of beasts had rushed towards him. She was looking down at him. When their eyes met, they smiled at each other. And with those smiles, their fears were kept at bay. They both knew that Zax would save them all.

Having surpassed everyone's expectations, including his own, they headed back to The Office to celebrate. Every agent who had been a part of this journey was there waiting, including Dr. Citlali and Agent Tonya, who had met Zax, Jaiden, and Jack at the gym. Even Dr. Reeves, the scientist who figured out how to recreate the beasts to their full potential, was there to join in on celebrating Zax's accomplishment. But no matter how confident or hopeful they appeared, each of them knew that this could be their last moment together.

Zax stood off to the side of the room while everyone else talked, laughed, drank punch, and ate pizza. Jaiden noticed him standing alone and walked over.

"Hey," she said.

"Hey."

"This reminds me of the second time we met," Jaiden said, leaning against the wall next to him.

"What do you mean?"

"In the cafeteria. When you were sitting off by yourself, separated from everyone else. Back then, you had a reason. Everyone made fun of you. But now you don't have to. Every person here cares about you and believes in you."

"Heh, I know. I just wanted to capture all of this from a distance, to see everyone at the same time," he said, scanning the room. "This. This is what I want to protect. All the people here who have done so much for me." He turned to her. "But most especially, I want to protect you."

Jaiden kept her eyes on the crowd, afraid that she would get emotional if she didn't. "I wanted to talk about the promise you made a few weeks ago. I think we should wait a bit longer for the marriage thing. I love that you promised to come back and that we could possibly even live together, but the marriage thing…I just want to wait."

Zax laughed, embarrassed. "Yeah. I got caught up in the moment. I'm sorry if I made you feel weird."

"No, you didn't do that at all! I want to be with you for the rest of my life, but we're just eighteen. Maybe in a few more years—"

"Ok, it's a deal. That way, we can have wine at the reception instead of punch." Zax swirled his drink as if it were a sophisticated glass of wine. They laughed at his quirky joke and then talked about everything from their past to what their future might look like when he defeated Dax.

Although everyone seemed to be having a great time, the party began to thin out as the evening wore on. Everyone there knew they needed to get home and prepare for whatever came next—be it the end of the world or the beginning of a new day. Whatever was to be, the time had come.

Jack went home for the first time in a while and thanked Mark for watching Sally at least a hundred times. Though he was going to miss the gym, he was glad to see his parents and Sally and sleep in his own bed. Zax dropped Jaiden off at her house and told her he loved her before heading home. Walter and Director Alvin stayed at The Office overnight.

The next day was going to bring an end to this conflict, once and for all. Regardless of where they were for the night, no one was going to sleep, knowing the Earth could be doomed if Zax failed.

53

The following morning Zax got to The Office before daylight. He was ready to go to Mount Everest and take down Dax. After handshakes and well wishes from those who came to see him off, he boarded the jet. The time had come.

"So, do you have a plan to force Dax into the core?" Walter asked, settling into his seat.

"Oh. I thought I mentioned it," Zax said anxiously, trying to get his seatbelt latched. "Well, I'm going to have to weaken him before I can do anything. But once I do that, I'm going to break through the top of Mount Everest and go down into the dormant central vent, forcing him further and further into the vent. From there, I'll push him through the crust, the mantel, and eventually into the core."

"Will you be ok, though?" Walter asked. "What if you get absorbed into the core as well?"

"Like you've said, Dax is only made of his energy. I have a physical body plus the energy. If I keep myself covered with a layer of an energy shell, my body should be fine." *Not a hundred percent sure about that, but I hope so,* Zax thought.

"I guess that makes sense." Walter noticed that Zax was rapidly tapping his foot. "Hey, there's no reason to be nervous. You've been training for the past month specifically for this. Just think of all the people you will save, all those who don't even know that this is happening. How about all The Office agents, Ethan, Jenny, and your friends Jack and Mark? And then there's the reason you have been fighting this entire time. The reason why you refuse to give up or lose. For Jaiden. I know you'll win, and Dax will know it soon too."

Zax nodded. Walter was right. He thanked Walter for the encouragement and for reminding him why he was doing this. Feeling slightly more at ease, he closed his eyes and tried to rest.

54

Walter and Zax arrived at the base of Mount Everest where a handful of office agents were already there and waiting. The agents had arrived days before to prep and clear a private, secretive landing strip—discovered by the same tech team who located the igloo—that had once been used by the local military. In order to maintain complete secrecy and overcome the treacherous weather, this was their only choice. The jet couldn't land any higher, and this was as close as they could safely get. Zax was going to have to make the trek to the thermosphere himself.

He geared up with the suit that Dr. Reeves had designed for him—the same suit he'd worn to the igloo in the Antarctic where he first encountered Dax—and disembarked into the brutally cold air. A few steps out, he stopped and turned around. Walter was standing at the top of the airstairs.

"Hey Walter, if I somehow fail or if I'm wrong about merging Dax with the energy in the core, I'm sorry."

Walter nodded. Zax turned back around and pulled the hood up over his head. The attached mask fell over his eyes. Then, without going into the aura mode, he blasted up. By using the energy around him to propel him forward rather than the energy required by the aura mode, he was able to conserve much-needed energy for battle. He went straight up the side of the mountain, faster than a rocket.

Zax flew faster than he ever had, yet the crisp cold air was only momentary. The cold air began to feel hotter and hotter as he rushed through the earth's lower atmospheric layers at unprecedented speeds. He had trained and conditioned his body so much that no amount of G-Force could affect him. Once he reached the exact height that Dax had defined, Dax was already there waiting.

"Did I keep you waiting long?" Zax asked sarcastically.

"Yes, actually. I have been waiting here the entire time."

"Let's get this over with. I promised some friends I would meet up with them after this encounter."

"I'll be sure and tell them you couldn't make it!" Dax said as he flew fiercely at Zax, initiating the battle. He was confident this would be over before it began.

But he was wrong. The second he started flying, Zax immediately shifted out of the way and Dax zipped past him, missing his target. Dax turned around, and with a shocked look on his face, he was confused by what had just happened.

"So, I see you've gotten even stronger," Dax said, regaining his composure. "Very interesting. I would say you might be half as strong as you were back before you became this chunk of rock."

"Dax, I have a proposition for you," Zax said unexpectedly.

"This isn't what I was expecting from you. But I'm curious. Continue."

"Let's not do this. What's the point of fighting this stupid battle?" Zax said. "This was a fight wagered billions of years ago. Don't you see? If the energy inside the earth were really serious about making the perfect planet, it would have destroyed the earth and moved on long ago. It was able to settle. Why can't you do the same on earth? You have a relatively normal human body. It's not like you can't."

"Are you so scared of me that you would rather beg me not to fight you? That you think I am going to let this blow over and try to settle? I am disappointed in you. I was trapped for *BILLIONS* of years in that damn prison, and you expect me to get over it just like that because I look somewhat human!"

"No, I'm far from scared. I know that if we fight, I will win. That's why I say we don't do this. You gave me a chance to get stronger and didn't hurt anyone during that time. You may act scary and heartless, but I don't think that's completely true. Maybe the actions the yellow energy took all that time ago weren't the best, and maybe it was being a tad greedy. But maybe it was also tired of seeing failed planets and knew it would fail if you used most of your power. Like you said in Antarctica, the planets that fell apart were the ones the yellow energy hated the most."

"I've heard everything you've been saying about me since The Glaze incident. How you'll kill me and make me pay for all the people that were slaughtered. So why the change of heart all of a sudden?"

"To be honest, I don't know myself. I thought about them…all the people who died and all the people who lost someone because of the violence. All that carnage was caused by your anger with the yellow energy and your overpowering desire for revenge. Then I began to think, maybe that's not how all those people want vengeance. First and foremost, I want all the violence to stop. Don't get me wrong, you *will* pay, but it doesn't have to be done through violence or killing."

"That is very touching and all, but while you represent determination, I represent power; I don't care about your words, only action!" Dax's voice boomed, and the ground beneath them shook.

"Fine, but I will get this done quickly. No more pain needs to happen today!"

"You're right about one thing. You won't feel any pain from how quickly I kill you!"

Dax disappeared and reappeared behind Zax. He did an uppercut, making contact with Zax's back. Purple sparks came from the point of impact and launched Zax higher into the air.

Zax quickly got his stability back. He rushed straight down toward Dax and stopped right in front of him. But before he could do anything, Dax punched him in the gut, not giving him a moment to act.

Acting like it hurt more than it did, Zax doubled over and moaned. A few seconds later, he raised his head and smiled devilishly at Dax. With a ball of energy in his palm, he pushed his hand forward and Dax's head blew off the energized form that made up his body. But it instantly grew back, the same as it had in Antarctica. Like nothing had happened.

Dax attempted to use an energy beam, much like the one he had used before, but Zax, doing nothing more than holding out his bare palm—without any energy— blocked the beam and protected himself. Zax then rushed towards him and let out a barrage of punches. Dax raised his arms in front of him, blocking most of the hits, but a few punches got through his defense and made contact with his body. Zax's fists were infused with the energy, and wherever his punches broke their way through Dax's defense and made contact, a chunk was taken out of his body. But just like when Zax blew off his head, the wounds healed themselves immediately.

55

As his body re-formed, Dax grabbed one of Zax's punches and hurled it back. The punch jabbed Zax in the chest and sent him flying backward. Instantly, Zax went into the aura mode. He made a broad sword out of his energy and swung the blade at Dax with a sideswipe. Dax made a shield out of the energy in defense, but the sword smashed it to pieces. Before the sword hit Dax, he grabbed the edge of the blade and pushed himself above into a barrel roll. Dodging it completely, he landed on the other side of the blade.

Dax punched in the direction of Zax. He tried to block the punch with the blade of the sword, but Dax's fist broke through the blade, making contact with his face and sending him flying again. Zax then made the deluxe broad quad star and threw it at Dax like he had with Professor Brian. It cut off Dax's left leg leaving the same energy barrier it had when Zax cut Professor Brian in two. But it didn't seem to matter. Dax's energy pushed through the barrier and grew back almost instantly, like all his other injuries.

"You know you can't beat me, right?" Dax said. "I'll just continue to grow back each time you injure me. There's only one way to beat me. Do you want to know what it is?"

"I already know. You have made so many mistakes. All this has just been child's play."

"Even if you do know how to beat me for good, you can't actually do it. I'm too strong for you to try," Dax laughed. "Don't you remember back in Antarctica? I can reuse my energy as much as I want, while yours just goes flying away until you get struck by lightning."

"Have you looked in the mirror?" Zax asked.

"What do you mean?"

"Your biggest mistake is choosing this place as a battlefield. It showed me exactly how to beat you and get rid of you for good!" Zax paused and stared at his enemy. "Oh, and one other thing. Have you noticed anything different about yourself?"

"What are you talking about?" Dax asked. Puzzled, he frantically started to look over his body. Then he realized what Zax was talking about. When the battle started, he was six feet tall. Now he was only five feet.

"How!" Dax yelled. "How is this possible!"

Zax smiled slyly. "One of your weaknesses is that your body is only made up of the energy. I have a physical body, which is what made me become stronger than you in the first place. You can't become any stronger than you already are. Like you said, you have all of your energy.

That puts a cap on how strong you can actually become. Unlike you, my energy grows with my strength.

"The other reason this is a bad battlefield for you is because we are practically on the edge of the atmosphere. After that is space. You know about that, huh? You were trapped out there, after all. You know…the place where stuff tends to drift off?

"All the times I have taken away parts of your body—parts of your energy—they have been drifting off into the abyss. About six months ago, The Office decided to make a satellite that could absorb any of my energy that got too close to the edge of the earth's atmosphere, traveling off path. Guess what? Your energy works the same way," Zax gloated with his devilish smile returning.

"So, I asked The Office director's son for a favor. I asked him to arrange for the satellite to be in this specific spot at this specific time. Now, I assume I'll just have to get you down to about three feet tall until you're weak enough to defeat."

Speechless, Dax looked at Zax with shock and fear. The only other time he had been outsmarted to this degree was when Zax's energy, the yellow energy, had defeated him millions of years ago.

Before he could respond, the star Zax had thrown earlier circled back like a boomerang and severed Dax's other leg. Zax disappeared and reappeared behind him.

With an axe kick to the top of the head, Dax plummeted down; more of his body was gone.

Zax darted beneath Dax and punched him back up with an uppercut. Then, with everything he had, he threw the deluxe spear at Dax and created a giant hole in Dax's chest. He delivered another deluge of energy-infused punches, taking away even more of Dax's body.

Although his body parts continued to regenerate, Zax continued getting shorter and shorter—four foot eight, four foot four, four foot two. Before Zax could shorten him any further, Dax broke free from his barrage and began to dodge and deflect Zax's attacks.

"I thought you were going to bury me up here on this mountain!" Zax taunted. "You can't do that if you keep evading me, can you!"

Dax was furious. *How did he get so strong and figure out how to defeat me so quickly!* he thought. It was happening all over again; he had gotten so cocky last time. Dax was certain he had won the battle all those years ago. That was until the yellow energy showed its ace in the hole. *If I'd just ended this back in Antarctica, we wouldn't be in this situation!*

Zax extended his right hand with his palm facing up, and multiple rings began to form. They hovered over his hand and began to rotate, each one in a different direction, like a gyroscope. The rings began rotating and spinning so fast that they took on the appearance of a solid ball. When they did, Zax forcefully flung it in Dax's direction. Seeing it coming, Dax ducked out of the way. But as soon as he moved, the gyroscope moved with him, and he took a direct hit to the chest.

"How is this happening!" Dax shouted again, doubling over.

"It's a gyroscope. It has something to do with measuring orientation or angular velocity. Physics stuff. Only this one detects and targets movement. So, if you move, it senses your movement, changes course, and comes directly for you."

Dax looked at the gyroscope ball suspended in front of him. Thinking he could escape another blow, he attempted to fly away. But the faster he flew, the faster the gyroscope ball flew. When it caught up with him, it whacked him back and forth, taking away more and more of his body. Once he reached three feet, Zax grabbed him by his jaw. He was now half the size of Zax.

Zax held Dax out in front of him and flew straight down. They crashed through the summit of Mount Everest and plunged into the dormant vent of the once-active volcano. Trying to squirm from Zax's grip, Dax seemed even more shocked by what was happening. Dax's shock confirmed to Zax that his theories had been correct; Dax did not know about the volcano. Tossing him in was the only way to defeat him.

56

Once they reached the base of the volcano, the temperature began to rise rapidly. It didn't take long for them to reach magma.

"What happened to 'no need for violence and killing!' You are just as bad as me if you go through with this!" Dax screamed in a last-ditch effort to save himself.

"I gave you a chance, and you threw it away! Plus, there is a big difference between fighting and hurting people simply because you can and fighting to protect the people you care about and everyone else on Earth!" Zax shouted. "You killed and injured all of those innocent people! You made the people I care about worry, and you threatened my planet! *NOW BURN IN HELL!!*"

"Damn it! Damn it! Damn it!" Dax raged as his mind ran rampant, clouded with confusion, and plummeted to his demise. *How? This cannot be happening!*

As they fell, Zax put an energy barrier around himself before they reached the very bright yellow energy core. He pushed Dax's body against the core and was thrust back. Dax started to sink into the core, and he knew history was repeating itself. He was slowly sinking into a prison. But this time, there would be no hope of return.

"YOU SON OF A BI…" Dax's final, angry words were interrupted by a roaring swirl as he was sucked into the energy.

Zax stared into the yellow core, a yellow abyss of power and energy. He had never seen it this close before. The only times he had ever seen this energy was when it talked to him in his dreams. He could only describe it as beautiful and frightening at the same time.

"I knew you could defeat Dax," a booming voice rang out.

Jolted from his gaze, Zax looked around to see if anyone else had shown up. Seeing no one, he realized this voice belonged to the energy.

"While you are here, you can ask me any question," it said.

Though Zax had many questions, he knew he did not have much time before his energy ran out and left him exposed to the surrounding lava. But there was one answer he had to know.

"Why did you choose me to have your power?"

"When you were a boy, before you lost your memories, you would do anything to make other people happy. You were incredibly determined to help as many people as you could.

"But one night, while you were riding in the backseat of your parent's car, they began bickering. Your father lost control, and the car went off the side of a cliff into a canyon. None of you survived.

"I saw your potential and gave you a greater piece of my energy than I had given to normal humans. It reincarnated you and gave you the powers you have now. When you use the energy, you can withstand it without having what humans call a heart attack because, technically, you are already dead.

"Now that I see you have mastered a portion of my power, I will give you the rest. I will swap my energy body—what you see in front of you—with something that can withstand this heat and pressure. With this power, you can change the world."

The energy started flowing toward Zax and was absorbed into his body. As this happened, Zax felt pure energy surge over, around, and into his consciousness, providing him with an undefinable feeling of power, peace, and stability. But the feeling was short-lived. He started to feel weak and knew he had to get out of the magma before he didn't have the strength to do so. He suddenly realized that absorbing the energy was more grueling and tiresome than he had initially thought.

"In due time, you will be able to call the energy back to you without having to recharge," the voice said.

Once Zax had fully absorbed the energy, nothing was left of the yellow energy but a solid chunk of iron. The battle was over.

Chapter 13
The Return

Dennis Eaves

Part 57

Zax flew out the same way he had entered, through the summit of Mount Everest. For a few moments, he hovered over the top of the mountain, his body getting weaker and weaker.

The battle had taken a considerably harder toll on him than he had expected; he was too weak and out of control to fly down. His body slumped and fell to the edge of a snow-covered slope, where he was knocked unconscious. The force of the impact created a major, thunderous avalanche. Zax was caught up in the churning mixture of snow and ice, traveling ever downward toward the base of the mountain. Twisting and tossing as he toppled, he finally dropped into a clearing near the base camp The Office had set up. When he regained consciousness and opened his eyes, Walter was by his side.

Walter yelled for the agents to bring a stretcher from the jet and had their on-field medic make sure he was safe to transport.

"He'll live. That much is for sure," Dr. Greene said as he began repacking his medical bag.

Relieved, Walter sighed heavily. "Good. Let's get him back to The Office so we can recharge him and get him back to normal. Come on, let's get out of here. We need to get Zax back home."

58

Back at The Office thirteen hours later, agents rushed Zax into the recharge room so that his injuries would heal quickly and his energy and stamina would be replenished.

Once the tesla coils shut down and he started to get up, Zax continued to feel weak. He realized how much of a toll the battle and absorbing all the energy from the center of the earth had taken on his body. He needed every last drop of the energy from the recharge—including what The Office had in their reserves—to come together. Even though the recharge brought back his stamina, he was still not a hundred percent.

Noticing he was unsteady on his feet, Walter and Director Alvin rushed in and grabbed his arms, helping him into the room with the monitor. Everyone was there. Jack, Mark, Jenny, Ethan, Dr. Reeves, Dr. Citlali, and Jaiden. Even Sally, since Jack didn't want to leave her home alone again.

"Zax!" Jaiden said as she ran to him with open arms and hugged him tightly.

The second she touched him, all his energy was totally restored. He lifted her up and twirled her around. *I did it! I was able to protect them. All of them, including Jaiden!*

When he put her down and heard the applause from the people he loved most, he was overcome with emotion. He fell to his knees and began to cry.

Jaiden got on the floor beside him and pulled his head into her shoulder. "It's going to be ok," she whispered, holding him close. *This must have gotten to him a lot more than he let on.* "I'm here for you, Zax. We're all here for you."

Just then, Jack picked Zax up by the back of his suit, and with tears in his own eyes, he gave Zax a long hug. "So glad you made it, buddy," he said. When they stepped back from the hug, Jack sniffled. And with a smile, he said, "Now tell us everything. It's got to be one hell of a story."

Zax wiped the tears from his eyes and ran his hand through his hair. "It is."

59

Zax sat at the head of The Office's small conference room table and told them everything about the battle, beginning to end. In great detail, he even explained the expression on Dax's face when he realized he was going to lose.

But within moments of finishing his story of the battle—before he could explain what happened between himself and the energy that was once in the Earth—the entire office building began to shake.

"Earthquake!" Mark shouted.

"That's not possible! We put The Office here because there were no fault lines," Director Alvin said.

Walter ran over to the computer and pulled up a screen that pinpointed the location of the disturbance. It read "THE CORE." What was happening at The Office was happening all over the planet.

"This doesn't make any sense; the core cannot shift like tectonic plates," Walter said.

"Did you not defeat Dax?!" Ethan yelled, turning to Zax.

"I did. This has to be something else...I can't feel Dax's power like usual!"

Behind them, Dr. Citlali turned on the television.

"I come to you live with breaking news from the western shore of America where there seems to be an island emerging from the ocean," reported an unfamiliar helicopter journalist.

"The merging with Dax and the core must have made changes to the Earth!" Dr. Reeves exclaimed.

"Dr. Reeves is correct. It is the only explanation." Horror-stricken, Dr. Citlali concurred. "Mixing dark power with light power must have done something, especially since the two powers combined in the center of the planet."

"Yeah. It could be that...or it could be that the energy in the core was absorbed into my body and replaced itself with a big chunk of iron," Zax said.

Everyone turned to look at him. "What?" They all said in varying tones and pitches.

"I'll explain later."

Straightaway, the shaking stopped. The island had stopped rising, but something else, something more unnerving, was unfolding.

An unknown creature jetted past the helicopter at breakneck speed. It passed with such force that the aircraft tumbled through the air toward the ocean. But with three yards to spare before crashing, the pilot regained control. The helicopter was not its target.

The creature continued flying until it reached its destination. It landed on the newly formed island. The cameraman in the helicopter had reestablished a visual of the creature. It had scales, a tail, and massive wings—the characteristics found only on a dragon. Out of the corner of his eye, he noticed something else. Tilting the camera up to the sky, he focused in on a purple and yellow swirling portal where more and more dragons were emerging. Lots more.

"Could the intensity of our energy clashing cause some other realm or portal to form?" Zax said.

"It would appear so," Walter said weakly.

As everyone stared at the monitor, speechless, Zax had one thing on his mind. *I thought this would be the end. But is it actually just the beginning?*

Epilogue

It had been half a year since the event that people called "The Unnatural" had occurred. Not long after The Unnatural events took place, Walter's father retired, and Walter was named the new director of The Office. After months of deliberation, Walter decided to release most of the top-secret information about the events surrounding Zax's battle with Dax.

The release told the story of Zax and everything that had transpired for the past year and a half. It explained how, according to Dax, the world came to be. The announcement summarized the events surrounding the battle between Zax and Dax and attempted to explain scientifically why The Unnatural happened. Some people believed the story; others did not and cried foul.

Within the political turmoil that followed, a new government was formed. Comprised of the best leaders from around the world, this new government created a special branch to oversee everything connected to The Unnatural, and Zax was appointed director. Though this officially ended his plan to work at The Office, he remained friends with Walter and maintained his affiliation with the agency. A major portion of their work was now focused on studying and monitoring the islands that had popped up in the Pacific. Of significant concern were all the new creatures that mysteriously roamed there. These creatures were now called Mythics.

With the arrival of the Mythics, who knows what the future will bring?

About the Author

Dennis Cazie Eaves is a sophomore at Piedmont Community College in Yanceyville, NC. In addition to writing and attending college, he volunteers at the local library, where he hosts an anime club and teaches Japanese calligraphy.

In 2021, while a senior in high school, Dennis published his

first book, *Zax and the Three Beasts*. With the publication of his second book, *Zax and Dax*, he is currently working on the third book of the Zax trilogy. To learn more about Dennis, check out his website, denniseaves.com, his author page at leastreetpress.com, or contact him directly at authorzax@gmail.com. You can also follow him on Instagram @zaxauthor.

Author of:

Zax and the Three Beasts

Zax and Dax

Coming Soon

Book Three of the Zax Trilogy